Sweetheart's Treats

THE COMPLETE SERIES

C.M. STEELE

THE STEELE PRESS

ISBN: 978-1-954645-11-0

Cover design: Bookin' It Designs

Sweet Surprise

Introduction

When Amelia arrives at work, she doesn't expect anyone but the owner of Sweetheart's Treats Bakery to be there. However, the sexy man in the kitchen is definitely not Carly. As the daughter of the sheriff, she calls the cops like she's been trained to do. Running would be another option, especially when she's spotted. Oops. Frozen in place, she's caught.

Blake is trying to figure out how to hold down the fort until his little sister gets better. She's been hit with the flu, and he wants to help. What he never planned for is to be immediately taken by his sister's employee. Unfortunately, nothing worth having comes easily. And Blake knows Amelia is worth everything.

Cupid's arrow seems to live inside Sweetheart's Treats. ***This is the first novella in the Sweetheart's Treat Series***

Chapter One

Amelia

It's February first and I've just started working for Sweetheart's Treats about a month ago. It's the only bakery in our small town of Palace, Texas. The owner, Carly, is a total sweetheart, hence the name of the shop. Her parents paid for her to start living her dream.

My dad is a great man, but there's no way in hell he has the ability to give me something like that. I'm at a community college because money is scarce. My dad, Derek Wright, happens to be the sheriff. He's been on his own since my mom abandoned us when I was two. He does what he can for me, but we're in a small town and his salary isn't great.

I reach for the handle and tug on the door, but it doesn't give. *It's locked.* That's surprising because Carly should already be here, and she never locks it since she knows I'm coming.

I call her, but it goes to voicemail. I step back and notice none of the lights are on. With my hands shielding my eyes, I press my face to the glass of the large picture window. I can see a man through the slightly open kitchen door. Immediately, I call my father.

"Dad, Carly's not answering her phone and there's a man in the kitchen. I can't get in, but all the lights are off."

"Get back in your car and wait for me." His voice is hard because he's worried. "Do not try to make contact."

Too late. The man's eyes dart toward mine, staring at me through the window. They are bright, but because of the morning sun glaringly pounding on the glass, I can't make them out. He throws me a quirky smile. I jump, gasping, and drop my phone.

If I wasn't staring, I wouldn't have been spotted. That can't be good if he's a thief. I step back and look down at my phone that's lying face up on the ground. Thankfully, it's it in an OtterBox case. It may have been a lot of money, but I'm clumsy so it's definitely worth it. The last phone and insurance cost me more. Lesson learned, but now I don't think it matters. I need to run, but I'm standing there like a fool.

"Amelia, Amelia," my dad hollers through the phone. I scoop it up just as the front door opens.

I freeze with my eyes trained on the intruder. A ridiculously fine one at that. Holy shit, the man's fucking hot as hell. He has short, light brown hair, and those eyes that penetrated through the glass with a devilish stare are a bright greyish-blue. He crosses his arms, leaning against the open door, smiling at me. I'm still standing there with my phone in my hand, admiring his strong arms instead of making a break for it.

"You're Amelia, aren't you?" he asks. He knows my name, and I'm trying to breathe because my heart is going wild and my insides are a mess. "I'm Blake Reynolds, Carly's brother. Please come in."

"Amelia," my phone says. *Wait, it's my dad, and I totally forgot about him.*

"Dad, sorry about the false alarm. It's Carly's brother." My dad starts to say something, but I miss it because Blake steps away from the door and takes the phone.

"Sir, my sister is sick and asked me to look after the shop. You know that the flu is going around and unfortunately, she's got it." He holds the door open, tilting his head for me to enter. I go in, feeling ill at ease about it. Not that Blake gives me a bad, dangerous vibe, but because I might make a total ass of myself.

He's so freaking fine that I am panting and mentally picturing his moving lips on mine. I'm so focused on them that I don't hear what he's saying to my dad. He ends the call, locks the front door again, then walks towards me with his brow cocked.

The look on his face makes me nervous. His stare commands me to keep my eyes on him. He cracks a smile, but there's a seriousness to it. He places a hand on the counter and leans in inches from me. "Amelia, don't stare at me like that or you're going to make me a liar."

"A liar?" I ask, stepping backward, hitting my thigh on the edge of the counter. It stings, but I ignore it.

He shakes his head at me. "Yes. Your daddy told me that I better keep my hands off you. And those lips of yours are tempting me more than a kid with a chocolate cake."

"Why would he tell you that?" I ask. He only says that to boys who want to take me out. He's ruined a lot of dating opportunities over the years. I've never had more than a kiss before. Sexy Blake wants to kiss me.

"Because...he's a dad. I'm sure I'll be that way when we have daughters. Seeing how he's the sheriff in town, I'll try to keep my hands off you for the time being." I'm stunned because he's like super-hot, and I'm pretty sure he just referred to having babies with me. Shaking my head, I clear it.

"When is Carly coming back?" I hope it's soon.

"I don't know. She's got a bad case of the flu. They took her to the hospital Saturday night."

I gasp. "Oh no, is she okay?"

"She will be. She's normally as healthy as an ox," he says with a shrug, turning around and moving to the back. Damn, does he have a nice ass. He's wearing a pair of jeans that hug it and a dark green cardigan sweater with a white dress shirt underneath. The man is a live model. I'm mentally drooling. I pause to check my chin to see if I actually am leaving a puddle around on my face, and thankfully it's all clear.

"I'm sure she wouldn't appreciate the ox reference," I reply, following him to the back. There's a lot of things to do before the shop opens in twenty minutes as nothing is ready to display. Normally, Carly has the first round of baked goods coming out of the oven by now.

"Well, that's what happens when you have a bratty little sister," he tosses out, grabbing his coat.

Leaning against the oven with my arms crossed, I question, "Is that something all brothers say?"

He's midway through putting his coat on when he asks, "Why? Do you have any that need their ass beat for calling you names?"

"No. I'm an only child, but it's common with my friends." He finishes sliding on his coat, and damn, he looks sexy in it too. It's a shorter-length leather jacket and fits him perfectly.

"I love her anyway. She begged me to come in, so I did. I'm keeping the shop closed for the morning so the cleaning crew can disinfect the place, but fuck if I know how to bake. That's where you come in, my princess. Carly told me you can do it," he says, reaching for my hand and giving it a squeeze. He needs to stop touching me because I can't think when he does.

Shit. I'm nowhere near as good as Carly. She has the skills and went to school for it. The shop opened a month ago, and this is my first baking job. As soon as the opportunity came up, I jumped on it because my old boss at the store wouldn't quit hitting on me.

Tyler stops in once a week, and luckily Carly deals with him while sending me to do something in the back. He's obsessed, and I regret that I haven't told my father about it yet.

"You can bake, right?" he asks, looking down at me. He actually towers over me because he's freaking tall. Well, since I'm short, most people are to me, but he's at least a foot taller than me. He's waiting for an answer, smirking at me in growing anticipation.

"Sure, but I can't design like Carly, and I don't have all the recipes memorized," I explain. I'm not what the town is expecting; then again, people don't want a side of the flu with their cupcakes.

"Princess, you got this," he says before taking my hand and leading me out the back door.

Chapter Two

Blake

I'm staring at my future. For the first time, I'm glad Carly got sick. I might have been playing it off, but I was worried about her. Helping at her shop was the last thing I wanted to do, but she loves this place.

I had no idea that her new employee would be my future wife. She's more beautiful than I could have imagined. Standing in the middle of my sister's shop with her light winter coat on and her dark brown hair in a messy bun, she anxiously awaits what I have to say. She'd been so busy staring at me through the window that she didn't realize her fate was sealed.

Her dad will be a problem, but only until she takes my name. He loves her, and I know when it comes to moving to Houston, he may not be thrilled. There's just one thing about it. I'm not leaving Palace without my princess.

"We'll wait outside for the cleaning crew. I don't want you to catch anything," I admit. Thinking of her getting sick feels like a punch to the gut. She's so much smaller than me and could fall deadly ill if she got sick.

"I work with her every day except on Fridays when she volunteers at the hospital children's wing. I'm not going to get sick," she contends.

That's where they think she caught it, but since she was here Saturday, I'm not taking any chances. I'm not afraid of getting it myself, but getting a customer sick could be a serious business killer. I lead her to where my truck is parked. The crew shows up as soon as I open my door.

I close it again and walk toward the back of the shop. "I'm going to give them directions, and then we can go to the diner across the street and talk while they clean."

"Did you make sure there's no money lying out?" she questions, like I'm just going to leave my sister's money lying around.

I shake my head in incredulity. "Of course, Princess. That's what I was doing when someone called the cops on me," I toss out, partially smiling as I faux scowl.

"Sorry about that." She blushes, dipping her head apologetically. God, she's so cute. I can't tell if she's normally this shy or if I'm making her this way. She has a little feistiness to her, but then suddenly it's gone, so betting it's the latter.

"No, you did the right thing," I say, tipping her chin to look at me. Damn, she's perfect. I want to kiss her, but I know it's not the right time. I need her to do her job for my sister. If I cross that line and she quits, Carly will never speak to me again. More importantly, I'll lose the woman I want to be my wife.

"Are you Mr. Reynolds?" a small woman in a parka asks.

"Yes. I need the entire place cleaned down and disinfected in the next three hours," I tell her. I don't care what her name is, but she hands over a business card that says it's

Denise Moreno. "Is that feasible?" I know it's a last-minute job, but they claim to be one of the best.

"Yes, sir." I let them in and give them some instructions before taking Amelia by the hand and leading her across the street. We get to the curb when the sheriff's car pulls up. I turn around and he hops out, eyeing me with deadly intent.

Amelia stills beside me, letting go of the hand I'd been holding. "Dad, what are you doing here? I thought you knew it was a mistake."

"Sweetie, when he tells me that you're going to marry him one day, I have to make sure you're safe." She directs her eyes to me, giving me an eye roll before turning back to her dad.

"I am, even if he's delusional," she informs him with a bit of sass. Oh yeah—she's not normally shy. I bring it out. I kind of like that. He grumbles something, then gives me another scathing look.

It seems to irritate him even more. "Doesn't look like it. You should be inside working, not being led away by some man."

I'm stepping in because even though I know he's trying to protect her, he's treating her like an imbecile and I don't appreciate it. "Sheriff, I'm having the shop cleaned right now so there are no traces of the virus. Amelia and I are going to eat breakfast and discuss the shop until they're done. You're more than welcome to join us."

There's a bit of pause as he considers my motives. "No, I have to go back." He narrows his gaze, staring me down with intent, jabbing his finger into my chest. "But I'm warning you that she's not to be played with."

"Sir, I don't play around. And one day, you'll see that," I answer. I might not appreciate being jabbed in my chest, but this man loves his little girl and I think he's grown accustomed to scaring boys away. The thing is, I'm a man.

"I better." He gives her a hug before leaving. I watch the obvious affection between them and know that at least she's been loved all her life. I'm going to continue that. Never has anyone made me feel this way. It's more than just infatuation, but I'll take the time to prove that to her.

"Wow, you can hold your own," she mutters, staring at me in surprise.

I look down on the itty-bitty brunette with a smirk, dying to kiss her but I hold back. "That I can, but it's what I do for a living. I'm the negotiator in the family company." I grab the door and hold it open for my princess.

"What is the family company?" she asks, walking into the restaurant.

"Printing and signage." I follow behind her, taking in her sexy ass. Even in her coat, I can make out her curves. I ache to hold her.

"So, you make the deals?" she questions, looking at me over her shoulder.

"Yes, Princess, and I'm going to make one with you. We enjoy breakfast and talk about Carly's shop, and you promise to celebrate Valentine's Day with me."

"What makes you think I don't already have a boyfriend?" she argues, taking a seat in a booth with the bakery in full view. I climb in on the other side so I have an excuse to stare at her the whole time, although I'd love for her to sit on my lap. The waitress hands us the menus and walks away with a laughing grin, which makes Amelia blush and focus on her menu. I pull it down to the table, forcing her to look at me. "Princess, your father is a bulldog. From what I can see, it's not likely. So...what about my deal?"

"That's fine. It's not like I'll be doing anything anyway,"

she says, shrugging her shoulders as if she's unaffected by me. I let go of her menu so she can hide behind it again. I already know what I want. I'm very hungry, and they have a big plate with it all including a T-bone steak.

Leaning back in my seat, I look around the room. We've caught the attention of several nosy-looking older women. Giving them a wink, I reach for Amelia's hand, intertwining her fingers with mine. Instead of pulling away, she leaves it for a minute until the waitress returns.

"I'll have the Man Breakfast Platter," I tell her, seeing her name tag and adding, "Thank you, Tracy." The woman isn't old, maybe in her early twenties, and is smiling at me as if I said she was the most beautiful woman in the world. I'm in no way interested in her, but I feel my princess eyeing me. I reach over and give her my full attention because even though I'm just being polite, Amelia is showing some jealousy.

Immediately, Amelia throws her order out, clearly annoyed by my civility to Tracy. "I'm going to have the over easy eggs and bacon with white toast."

"Coming right up. I'll bring you both some coffee," Tracy says. "Goodness, you did good, girl," she adds, patting Amelia's shoulder. A smile creeps across her face for just a second, but as soon as Tracy walks away, she directs her attitude to me.

"Now they think we're a couple," she complains as if she really minds. It didn't feel like it when she held my hand. I get that this is a small town so by tonight everyone will know, but it shouldn't be a problem.

"They should. I'm not settling for anything less." She deserves my honesty, but I need to slow it down.

"I thought you promised to talk about Carly's place, and not us?" she protests.

"I never said I wouldn't talk about us. But as promised, I want to talk about the work since we do have to open in a few hours and I'm not a baker."

"Do you think it'll be ventilated enough with the disinfectant?"

"It should be. They are wiping down things and mopping. I'm sure they'll be careful. Their resume says they do commercial kitchens."

She takes a sip of her water, then remarks, "Good, I'd hate to bake Pine-Sol-flavored cookies."

I hold back a laugh and shake my head. "Me too. So what kind of cookies and other sweets are you going to dish up?"

"I'll do as much as I can, but we have sheets of brownies to make along with different cookies. Brownies are our biggest sellers. People love the perfect number of nuts to chocolate combo. Right now, there's nothing ready to hit the shelves. Everything is baked fresh and never stays for more than forty-eight hours."

"I'll help all I can."

They brought our food to the table quickly, but she and I managed to devise a game plan for today before they set it down.

"So, I'm going to keep the shop open until seven as scheduled, but you'll be leaving to go to class by four, right?" It kind of messed with the plans I had in my mind for her, but it was nice to know she's trying to get an education.

"Yes, then tomorrow, I can be there at five to get an early start like your sister normally does."

"She needs to hire more employees. Aren't there any other girls in town looking for a job?" I see her eyes narrow at my suggestion of more women.

"Probably, but she likes to be hands-on all the time."

"Yes, but for instances like this and the next two weeks when it's insanely busy for Valentine's Day, who's going to handle all the chaos? That's why she got sick easily. Running herself ragged."

"I agree on the latter, but this town isn't overwhelmingly large, like Houston. It has a dozen streetlights."

"Still, if she had a backup, I wouldn't have to be here," I say. It's a terrible argument, and I realize it immediately.

"No, you wouldn't," she murmurs, taking a bite of her eggs.

"Then again, I wouldn't have met you either," I add. She's the best reason to be here.

Chapter Three

Amelia

He's trying to help, but he's completely in the way. "Why don't you set up the register so I can finish these," I tell him as I slide another sheet of cookies into the oven and take the brownies out to cool. Then I start to use the heart-shaped cookie cutter to make heart-shaped brownies. It's something that I hope sells. As I set up this morning, it came to me. Hopefully Carly doesn't get mad at me for it.

"I'm not any help, am I?" he asks, stealing one of the cookies I set out for display. I smack his hand, which shocks both of us. He's staring at me with those sexy grey-blue eyes.

"No, but I like having you around," I admit, swallowing hard. I finish up the brownie shapes, pretending that a jolt of electricity didn't course right through me from touching him.

He reaches out, brushing a strand of my hair out of my face and tucking it behind my ear. My heart purrs like the engine of a Hellcat. I know that if he kisses me, I won't stop him. I want it more than he does. My body yearns for him more than ever. The shivers running through me feel never ending. They travel all over, up and down my spine and going straight to my core.

"Stop being sweet Amelia because I'm going to kiss you." His voice is low, but the warning loud and clear.

"You make it sound like that's a bad thing," I whisper, looking up at him with his hand cupping my jaw. I clench my thighs to hold the intense feeling inside. He's focused on my mouth and I think the kiss is coming, but he shakes out of the mini-trance.

"It is because I won't be able to stop. And, it's almost time to open." He straightens up and takes the tray to set in the display cases. I breathe a sigh of relief that I have a minute alone. Not because he bothers me, but I feel so antsy and want to be wrapped up in his arms.

The bakery is in a small shop, but the entire perimeter of the room is full of standard food-display cases. The smell of disinfectant had faded a while ago. The smell of sweets and chocolate takes its place, making it almost divine.

Once I set the last tray in the case, I take a walk around the room to see if it looks pretty enough. And it does. We were supposed to put the decorations up today, but with Carly sick, I'll have to find some time to do it later. I move to the front door, unlock it, and flip the sign to open.

"Let the games begin," Blake exclaims, rubbing his hands together.

Three hours later, I'm back in the kitchen making the last batch of cookies and heart-shaped brownies. They are a big hit.

I have to leave in a few minutes to make it to school on time. I'm so tired already, and I still have a few hours ahead of me. It's been chaotic today. It was so busy that Blake and I could barely get a word in edgewise. It's never swamped like today. Maybe it's because the bakery opened so late, and everyone had questions about it being closed. They all gave their best wishes for Carly's health and return.

"Princess," Blake says, walking into the kitchen in a mad rush. "I know you're busy right now and leaving soon, but I have to do this." He pulls me away from the counter and closes his mouth over mine. I'm shocked and pleased, melting into his kiss. Our mouths are perfectly matched, gliding along one another, his tongue slipping inside my mouth, and I moan out.

It shakes him out of the moment, and he steps back. "Sorry, but damn, I'm going to need a minute." He walks into the office, leaving me standing there in surprise.

Shaking my body out of its daze, I return to work because we can't leave the store alone for more than a second today. I step out and Tyler's there, stealing that precious kiss from my mind. "Hello, Mr. Wills." He's looking at me the way he always does—leering and ogling my body. I shudder from his gaze.

"It's Tyler, Amelia. Why are you always playing hard to get? I know you're a sweet little virgin, but I can turn you into a woman," he offers, and I want to vomit. He's a good-looking guy, but I'm not interested and he refuses to listen. His attention only makes me sick to my stomach.

"Not if you want to live to see tomorrow," Blake says, walking up to my side and sliding his arm around my waist. Tyler's eyes don't miss the obvious sign from Blake. "Get out before I throw you out."

"This is interesting. We're not through, Amelia. You're mine." He storms out, and I can feel the tension rolling off Blake beside me, his hand tightening around my waist.

I move to get out of his arms so that we're standing in

front of each other. I already regret the loss of his arms, but I have to leave.

"You have a crazy ex?" he gets out through clenched teeth with one hand leaning on the glass countertop. I can see he's livid as he keeps darting his stare to the door, but he's got it all wrong. I brush my hand over his, which he takes and holds.

"No. He's never been my boyfriend, but he won't take no for an answer." It's been a hassle, nothing more. Today, though, it felt different. I'm actually scared that he'll do something now after seeing Blake.

"And your dad hasn't threatened him yet?" he questions. I pull away, biting down on my bottom lip because I know he's not going to like the next part. "What is it, Amelia?"

"I haven't told him," I stammer, sliding the cookies into their place in a hurry before trying to make a mad dash to the kitchen. He stops me with his arm slinking around my waist. I fall back, landing against his strong chest.

He spins me around to face him. With a fierce expression, he says, "That's not smart, Amelia. He's not going to innocently go away. What he said after being confronted didn't change his tone. That's not good."

"So, you're the expert on crazy when it comes to the opposite sex?" I argue.

"No, but I watch a lot of crime shows when I get home from work, and it's not good when there are guys like that." His expression softens, and I melt into his hold.

Our tender embrace lasts a moment before I realize that I'm running behind. "I don't have time for this. I have class in thirty minutes and need to get going."

"Shit, I'm sorry. I'll walk you to your car, and I expect

you to call me when you get out. And when you get home. Understood?"

"Yes, Blake. I promise." I gather my things as he handles two customers who came in while I was changing. Walking me to my car, he peers around, looking for Tyler. I hate that I know he's right.

He doesn't kiss me again, and I go to class feeling extremely lonely—something I've never really felt before.

Blake

I'm on my way to the shop before the sun's up because I don't want her to be there alone, and fuck if I don't miss her. I made a call last night and I'm sure if she found out she'd be pissed, but her dad had the right to know. He wasn't pleased, but I did earn a sliver of brownie points.

"Good morning, Amelia," I say as I enter from the back entrance.

She turns her head to me with a smile on her face. "Good morning, Blake. I didn't expect to see you here this early." God, she's so damn pretty. I want to greet her with a kiss.

"Why?" I told her that I wouldn't be letting her open by herself.

"I thought you said you had to attend a meeting this morning?" she reminds me.

"It's a conference call so I can take it from Carly's office." I take off my coat and head into the office. Just knowing she's safe is all I need for the time being. After my long talk with her father, I decided to take a step back; it's what's needed.

I don't want to push her into anything, and with that crazy fuck lurking, I didn't want to give him a reason to come harder after her. The sheriff has plans to catch him, and since he can make the call on her case, he will.

I help set up for opening, limiting our conversation to bakery business. After the conference call, I had to handle inventory and only asked her some basic questions.

She has to go to school before I know it. I walk her to her car and demand she calls me like she did yesterday. "Goodness, you sound like my dad." I'll let her make me a dad, but she has no idea that I'm doing all I can to hold back.

"Don't start. Have a good day at school. I'll see you tomorrow." I wait until she drives away before heading back into the bakery. My heart hurts a little bit each day. It sucks that I'm waiting it out, but as the changes for us will be permanent, I have to know she's sure of herself and us.

An hour later, Tracy comes into the shop. "Hi," I greet her like any other customer, keeping up the friendly service even though I'm missing Amelia.

"Wow, where's Carly and Amelia?" she asks, looking around the place.

"Amelia's at school, and my sister is out sick," I inform her. I assumed everyone knew about Carly already.

"Oh, so you know Amelia's dad's the sheriff, right?" she teasingly asks.

"Yes, I've met him already," I say, nodding and laughing.

"Good, because he usually pushes all the guys away from her. She deserves a good man, but the only one is her dad." I get the strange inkling she has a thing for the sheriff, and speak of the devil, he's entering the shop.

"Hello, Ms. Hope," he greets her, smiling and tipping his hat.

"Sheriff, when are you going to call me Tracy?" He ignores the question and turns to me. I don't miss the look of sadness she hid just as fast as she showed it.

"Blake, if you mistreat my daughter, I'll bury you. That includes flirting with Tracy." I bite back a laugh because he so wants her.

"Sir, I'm not the type to flirt with a woman when I have one. Now, is there something I can get you?" I ask, smirking at him.

"No, I came to check on things." He gives me a knowing look, and I get the message. He saw Tracy come in. And it's got nothing to do with Amelia. He wants her, but I can see it's probably the massive age gap stopping him. Maybe if she's with him, it would make the loss of Amelia to me in Houston a little easier.

"Good deal, sir." I look at Tracy and smile at her because it's clear as hell that he needs a push. "You know, Tracy, if you're looking for another job, I could use some help here. Amelia's at school in the afternoon."

"No, she can't do it. She's busy," the sheriff spits out.

Both of us look at him. She scowls, then turns to me and adds, "I'm not busy, Blake. The diner isn't open after four anyway, so I can certainly work here too."

"Great. Can you start now?" I add fuel to the fire.

"You bet," she cheers. I'm not sure if she's doing it to get at him, or because she needs the job.

The sheriff's radio goes off, but he doesn't answer it. It starts again, and he answers. "I'm watching you, Blake." He leaves, waving us off. I'm sure he's ready to lose his mind.

"Tracy, let's get you trained so that tomorrow you can come in and handle a lot by yourself."

"Thanks for giving me the job. I'm lucky places around here are cheap, or I'd be homeless."

"Is it that bad?"

"Well, I only work part-time at the moment. I'm ready to leave and go somewhere else. I have a side career, but it's more like a hobby."

"What is it?" I ask, making conversation.

"I'd rather not talk about it," she murmurs, blushing and ducking her head.

I shrug and add, "Well, if you need any help, let me know." I don't press because it's not a big deal to me.

We make it through the day, and I go to Carly's place because I need sleep painfully. Since having met Amelia, I haven't slept a lot, so I quickly pass out and forget about everything but rest.

I don't wake up until four in the morning, missing Amelia's calls. I feel like a dick and rush to the bakery before she gets there.

I beat her there and try to get things started. The doorbell rings, and it's the delivery truck. I take the ingredients inside and then Amelia arrives.

"Good morning, Blake," she mutters in obligation rather than with joy. I see she's mad, and I'm feeling shitty about it. Something could have happened to her last night, and I wouldn't have known.

"Morning, Princess," I grunt as I pick up the three twenty-five-pound bags of flour and carry them into the kitchen.

"So, my dad says Tracy's working here now." I hear the accusation in her voice, but I carry on because I know she's not done.

"Yes, we could use some help around here. And she came in at the right time," I reply, brushing off her attitude.

"Explains why you didn't answer my calls last night."

I drop the bags down onto the back counter and rush to her. Grasping her around the waist, I lift her off her feet and then set her ass on the other counter, standing between her legs. "I'm sorry I didn't answer, and that's why I'm here early. I haven't slept since we met, and my body called the shots. I didn't wake up until four, then I rushed to get to you. I'm sorry. You're jealous, and I get it, but you've got nothing to feel that way about."

"Then why did you eagerly hire her?" she asks, jabbing me in the chest.

"I told you we need help. I have another job, and this bakery is added stress. Besides, she's perfect for the place. She's nice, polite, and has great customer service skills. And..." I stop myself because I don't know how she feels about her father falling in love again. It wouldn't be my place to tell her about the connection I saw between them.

"And what?" she asks, arms folded, trying to create some distance between us.

"Nothing. It's time to get to work. I have another meeting today and will have to leave for a few hours."

"Oh, no conference call?"

I run the back of my hand down the side of her neck to the pulse at the edge of her V-neck top. "No, Princess. I have to be there for it, but don't worry—you're safe."

"Safe?" she asks like she doesn't have a fucking stalker.

"I have someone looking over the place. He won't let him anywhere near you."

"You've hired someone to follow me?"

I'm not going to fight about having security. "No, just to look after you when I'm not around. You won't see him because I don't want his ass anywhere near you, but he's here to protect you. Don't argue with me. Just nod your pretty head, or I'm not going to let you down."

"You're infuriating," she mutters, annoyed but with little to no conviction.

I slam my hand to my chest dramatically. "You wound me, my princess. I'm supposed to be your knight. Let me be." She hesitates for a moment before she nods in agreement, and I can't stop myself. I close the distance and thrust my hands into her long, dark hair and crush her mouth to mine. It's been so long since I've felt her lips on mine and I'm not sure I'll ever let go.

She throws her arms around my neck, and the kiss grows, intensifying as she wraps her legs around me. I'm grinding against her core as she moans. I pick her up and hold her by her ass, rocking as we kiss.

"Wow, this is not what I expected to walk into," Tracy says. I slide Amelia down my body quickly. I'm hard as a rock, so I move to stand behind her.

"Sorry, it's not what you think," Amelia explains, smoothing down her hair and adjusting clothes back into place, looking everywhere but at me.

"Yes, it is," I tell her, giving Tracy a look of incredulity while wrapping my arm around Amelia's waist and slamming her against my body, letting her feel what she did to me.

"Well, I just wanted to see if you needed any help baking before I head across the street," Tracy says, clapping her hands on her hips.

"I'm sure she could use some. I'm going to handle setup. Ladies, holler if you need me." I kiss Amelia on the cheek and head to the door.

"Blake, can you please put the flour in the large

cupboard first?" Amelia calls out before I have the door halfway open.

"Of course, Princess. Anything for you." I whip a smile at her and move the bags.

The morning goes by fast and I'm off to my meeting. I hope I'll be back before Amelia goes to class, but I don't know how long it's going to last. The guy I'm going to see is a talker.

Chapter Five

Amelia

Working with Tracy has been great. I'm somewhat over the jealousy thing after Blake did all he could to show me that I'm his. Tracy's pretty and young, and maybe a bit closer to Blake in age. Still, she doesn't seem interested in him which is a good thing because I'd pull her pretty hair out. In fact, several guys in town took notice of her, but she brushed them off.

"It's almost time for me to go," I tell her, taking off my apron. The store has been so busy that I've hardly had five minutes to miss Blake, but every one of those was filled with a painful sadness.

"Do you go to school every day of the week?" Tracy asks, organizing the last of the cookies and brownies on the shelves. We have more in the oven, and they have been selling faster than normal. I think it's because more people are aware of the bakery and coming for treats. Blake's right; Valentine's Day is going to be jam-packed.

"Yes, I wanted to get all the classes I could in at one time."

"That's got to be tiring." I'm about to answer when the door chimes. Both of us look up to see my dad strolling in. He looks around the room as if searching for someone, which I suspect is Blake.

"Dad, what brings you here?" I ask, coming from around the counter for a hug. He returns it, but I see that his attention is drawn away from me for a second. It comes back, but I know what I saw. A beeping comes from the kitchen. "Oh, hold on, I need to get the brownies."

"I can do it," Tracy offers.

"No, you've done a lot today. I'll get them." I rush to get them from the oven and let them cool. When I come back out, I see that I've missed something. The room is heated with tension, and they both look upset.

"Can I get you anything, Dad?"

"No. I just wanted to walk you to your car. I know that's for your boyfriend, but he's apparently not reliable." My dad has been this way any time a guy shows me interest, but the thing is, Blake's the only one I didn't want him to push away. My heart belongs to Blake already. I can't even fathom the thought that Blake would cut his losses.

"Dad, that's not fair. Blake is at a business meeting for his real career. He's been nothing but respectful and sweet."

"Sorry. You're my baby girl, and I want the best for you."

"I understand, but I'm old enough to make my own decisions," I remind him.

He grumbled and then threw his hands up in surrender. "Fine. I'll try to cool it. Well, are you ready?"

"Do you have this until Blake gets back?" I ask Tracy. I'd hate to leave her alone because I can't help but think of Tyler's visits.

"Sure. Good luck at school and with him," she tilts her

head toward my dad. They don't say bye to each other, and I wonder if it's my imagination or if they're fighting the insane heat between them. Maybe I'll try to ask my dad about it later.

I let his bad attitude go with the others, but I have to put my foot down where Blake's concerned. I want him more than I want to breathe, and it hurts to be away from him. "Dad, I know you don't want me to find anyone," I blurt out, unsure of where I'm going with this.

He stops on the pavement while I walk to my driver's side door. "Wait right there, young lady. I do want you to find someone. I just want to know that he's good enough for you and willing to put up with a lot to have you. When your mother walked out, I was young too, but she couldn't handle when things got tough. She wasn't ready to be a mother, and although I wasn't to be a father either, I never stopped wanting you. You've been my life for so long that I don't want that to happen to you. Hell, even now I'm still learning and not even sure what I'm getting at. I know Blake's a good guy, but I'm a dad. It's my job to worry."

I get in and lower the window. "I'm fine, Dad. We don't even see each other outside of the bakery, but he made me promise to go on a date on Valentine's Day."

"That's going to be nice." I nod, then start my engine. It takes two times for it to turn over. "You need to get this hunk of junk into the shop."

"I think so too, but I don't have time right now." With school, homework, and actual work, I can't afford to go without a car for a week. It's not that it's bad, it's just the middle of winter and it's an older car. It takes more to start it when the weather is less than perfect. We're just north of Houston, and this winter has been unusually cold. My poor baby is a warm-weather beast.

"Make sure it happens soon," he scolds me.

"Yeah, yeah, yeah," I agree, rolling my eyes in the process before shifting the car into drive.

"Do you like this guy?" he asks in a hurry to get an answer out of me.

"I really do." It's more than that, but that's all I'm going to tell my dad. So, I pull out, leaving him standing at the curb.

As I pull up to the first stop sign, I gasp. Leaning on the streetlamp, Tyler is staring at me. He opens his coat just enough for me to see that he's carrying. I would have peeled out already if it wasn't for old Mrs. Jenkins crossing with her cane. The moment she gets two feet away from my car, I hit the gas and drive to class.

My mind knows it's not a coincidence, but in order to keep myself sane, I spend the rest of the evening lying to myself that it was just a mere run-in. After all, our town is small and Tyler works nearby.

Chapter Six

Blake

A week has passed since I met Amelia. The shop was opened over the weekend, but I had to go back to Houston on Sunday to play catch-up. I wanted to ask Amelia to come with, but I promised to give her time. I enter the shop ready to work, but Amelia has taken advantage of the warm front.

Today's high is seventy-five, and she's in a blue paisley skirt that just flows above the knee. She's wearing a tight top that hugs her slender waist and breasts. They bounce when she spins toward me. "Good morning, Blake," she sings, smiling up at me.

"Damn right, it is." Closing the distance and slipping a hand in her pinned up hair with my other arm around her waist, I crush her mouth to mine and kiss her like we both need. I've avoided touching her since Tracy walked in on us, but that time is over. Tracy's off today. I've got time to touch my princess.

I pick her up, and she wraps her legs around my waist. I carry her into the office because I'm not letting this go with just a kiss. I sit her on the desk, thankful that I'm neat and it's almost clear.

"Blake," she moans, thrusting her hands into my hair and grinding her hips. Pulling back, I slowly creep my hand up her thigh until I reach her mound. Her panties are soaked as I stroke her over the material, over and over.

She cups my head and kisses my neck, moaning and crying for release. I slip my fingers under her cotton panties, rubbing her core, teasing her drenched hole. Needing to hear and feel her explode just for me, I push one into her pussy. My thumb brushes her sensitive clit, and my woman comes on my hand. I'm so hard that I can't think straight, but I pull back and fix her skirt.

"Did I do something wrong?"

Nudging her nose with my own, I promise her, "No. God, no, but if I keep touching you, I'm going to fuck you right here and now, and that's not how our first time should be."

I leave the office and go straight to the bathroom. I whip out my cock, and with thoughts fucking her right on the nearest surface, I come with three fucking strokes. After I clean myself up I come back, and she's shyly working again.

She turns away from me to focus on her task, but I can read her. Sliding up behind her, I whisper, "Don't worry, Princess. I'm going to love you right as soon as possible."

"I want it, too, Blake," she whispers as she puts the next tray into the oven. I take out two cookie trays while she gets the rolls.

It's time to open, and a line of customers is forming. There's going to be no time for talking before the day is through. It's been rough because this whole week I've had to split my time between running the managing aspect of the bakery along with my actual job, when really all I want to do is spend it with Amelia. We make it through the day before she has to leave for school. Now I've missed her uncontrollably, and it shows.

I get to Carly's and sit on the sofa. I know Amelia will be calling any minute now, and I can't wait to hear about her day.

It's been a long, tedious day without seeing her as much as I wanted to. "Hey, Princess. How was school?" I ask as soon as I pick up the phone. We had a brief minute alone, and it got heated. I pulled back the moment she came, but we spent the day eyeing each other with intent. I pictured different positions several times around the shop.

"Good, I'm getting home right now. I have to start dinner. Do you want to come over?"

"Are you inviting me to dinner?" I ask. My voice gives away my shock. After this morning, I thought she understood any alone time together was going to end with me inside her.

"Yes. Why do you sound surprised?"

I'm checking my appearance in the mirror before leaving. I look good enough, so I don't waste time getting ready. Having Amelia in my arms is all I desire. I'm not even hungry. "It's just a sweet surprise. I've been giving you time to come to terms about our future."

"And what would that be? I believe we have a date, but that's about it."

"We're going to have way more than that. Soon, you're going to be my wife and carrying my babies," I growl into the phone as I hop into my truck.

"You know just kissing doesn't get you there," she reminds me. I'm doing all I can to drive safely, but this woman is pushing my limits.

"No, but fucking you on my sister's counter or desk isn't quite romantic or sanitary, and I've been so damn close that you'd have chocolate in your pussy if I got my way."

"It definitely would be one hell of an experience," she replies.

My dick is harder than stone at the moment thinking about eating chocolate out of her sweet pussy. Fuck, I struggle, but I get it together enough to focus on the road.

"Is your dad home?" If he is, this will be a long night. If not, I hope it still will be, but for a different reason.

She giggles before saying, "No, he's on his overnight shift. He left about fifteen minutes ago. You have me all to yourself."

"You know I'm already on my way to your place. You better be careful, or I'm going to fuck you on the nearest surface." I've been good at giving her space. Our kisses at the bakery have been few and far between, but every time, they were intense. This morning, we pushed the limits and now there's no going back. The genie is out of the bottle.

"Good, because I've been waiting for so long." I hear the desire and longing. I'm going to come before I get inside her. I pull into her driveway and rush up the stairs. She opens the door and runs into my arms.

"I missed you, Princess." I carry her into the house, closing the door with my foot. "Bedroom?"

"Upstairs to the left," she moans against my mouth.

I manage to find her room and set her on her feet. My hands go to the hem of the skirt she's been tempting me with today. My hands thrust under her and I cup her ass. She's not wearing panties, and that is hotter than I could imagine. Squeezing her soft cheeks, I pull her against my cock.

"You're mine, Amelia. Are you ready for me?" I rub my

length on her, letting her know what's to come. She moans, her hands tugging on the hem of my shirt, yanking it from my pants.

"Yes, I am, Blake. Please. I need you to take me," she pants. Her chest rises and falls.

"There's no going back. There's no nothing going on. We're getting our fucking happily ever after. You understand me?"

"I want it, too. Give me everything you can," she cries out. I unzip her skirt, sliding it down her legs. Her pussy is on full display for me. Her lips glisten with her desire. I run my fingers along her seam. I want inside her one way or another, any second now.

I remove my hand long enough for her to lift my shirt over my head and me to do the same to hers. She's standing in front of me completely naked. I stroke myself once. My cock is still trapped in my pants, but I'm too greedy to wait. I kick off my shoes as I walk her backward to the bed. The back of her knees hit the mattress, sending her ass to the bed. I lean over her until she's laying flat.

"I'm going to eat you up, Amelia. I want you to come for me before I take what's mine." My mouth waters as I lower myself. I roughly part her thighs and press my face to her slit. She pushes away, nervous about what I'm about to do. "Now, do you want to come or not, my princess?"

She nods, unable to speak. Her thighs are flexed closed.

I spank her pussy, ordering her, "Open." She complies, availing me to her perfect pussy. I watch her clench her core, but I'm not sure if she's eager or scared. I run my hands over her thighs until I reach her wet lips. My thumb rubs her little pearl, and her hips arch.

"Mine," I whisper lovingly before sliding my tongue

through her folds, lapping up her wetness while I glide one finger into her hole, pumping it in and out.

She comes for me, rocking her hips up and down. Fuck, I could eat her out all damn day, but another time. My cock is pulsing in my pants. I stand and pull them down along with my briefs. The tip is dark and angry looking. It's so damn hard, I don't know if I'll manage to last long.

She scoots to the center of the bed, resting her head on the pillows. She's no longer shy after seeing what she's done to me. I lick my lips and climb between her legs. My cock bobs on the mattress, leaving a drop of pre-cum on the sheets. Hope her daddy doesn't do the laundry.

"Are you ready?" I ask, rubbing my cock along her slit. It feels fucking incredible. The soft, welcoming wetness is too inviting. Leaning with one hand holding up my body, I line my cock up with her core and push slowly inside. She's tighter than I could even imagine. I close my eyes and attempt to relax.

Lowering my head to her perfect tits, I rub my jaw along her chest. My tongue peeks out, flicking her nipple before sucking hard. Her back arches and I thrust forward, claiming her for my own.

"Shit," I grunt, seeing the pain on her face. Her expression changes from a frown to a gentle smile as if she can read my fear. "I'm sorry. I'd hoped it wouldn't be too bad."

"I'm fine, Blake. Please don't stop."

I say a silent thank you because I didn't want to pull out, but I would if she asked. "I'm not, my princess."

I take a kiss, stealing her moans as I rock forward. Her hands release the sheets and slide over my ass. She squeezes and holds me in place, pushing my cock completely into her. I'm fully seated in her and stretching her while she clenches around me. Beads of sweat slide down my spine as I hold back from filling her depths.

"Fuck me, Blake," she demands.

Always obliging, I pump into her. Her nails dig into my shoulders, and it spurs me on. Needing her to come again, I move to tease her pussy with my hand. Hitting her nub with my thumb sends her over the edge. I give her two more thrusts before coming hard into her unprotected womb.

Drained, I collapse on her. Most of my weight is on her, but as I try to move, she holds my body to hers with her thighs wrapped around me.

I roll over and take her with me. We lay there, resting until there's a beeping noise downstairs. "Oh, shit. Dinner's done."

"I completely forgot about it. Let's get dressed and eat. Then I say we come back up here and you let me love you again."

"Sounds wonderful." She gets up and grabs her clothes before walking out of the room. I do the same and realize the bathroom is in the hall. Shit, I'm glad her dad's not home. I step out and walk to the bathroom to wash up. Amelia comes out as I go in, and I steal a kiss before taking my turn. As I step out I hear her scream.

I'm about to go downstairs when I see Tyler standing in the middle of the living room. He's got a gun pointed at my woman. I'm not concerned about me; all I can think about is getting her to safety. I creep down to the last step.

She's worried. I can see it in her eyes. He's so focused on her he didn't hear me or catch me in the periphery. Granted, I'm at the perfect angle, but I'm hoping he doesn't react before I can do what I'm planning.

I make enough noise that he turns the gun away from

her to see me just as I deck him in the jaw, but not before he gets a shot off. A burning pain tears through my arm. Fuck.

"Blake," she cries out.

Gritting my teeth, I manage to say, "Princess, go into your bedroom and lock your door. Call the cops. Hurry. Don't leave that room. I love you, Amelia." I continue to pummel the fucker, and the gun falls to the floor. He tries to go for it, but I cold-cock him again. This time his ass is knocked out, or so I think. He comes at me again, and I fire two shots to the chest and thigh. He hollers, and Amelia comes running down.

"I told you to stay upstairs," I snap.

"I heard him scream after the shots. I figured it was safe. They're on their way." She runs to me carrying towels in her hands and begins pressing them to my arm. Tyler's bleeding, but still alive. Good. I want him to rot in prison.

"You better not die on me," she sobs, holding my wound and kissing my forehead.

I laugh, and whisper, "Of course, my princess." I hear sirens in the distance, but I'm starting to lose consciousness.

Chapter Seven

Amelia

I can barely see through the tears as I rush to the ambulance. They are loading Blake inside, and he's not awake.

"Can I ride with him?" My dad nods to the EMT, who is my classmate's older brother, Felix, and he helps me in. We've become good friends over the years. My hands are shaking, but I need to believe Blake's going to be okay. It takes a few more minutes to stabilize him, and then they start to drive.

I can't stop touching him. My hands run along his chest. They've bandaged his arm, but they say he's lost a lot of blood. I'm trying not to panic, but I don't want to lose him.

"Amelia, he's going to be all right. You have to be positive," Felix says, placing his hand on my shoulder.

"It's my fault. He's shot because I invited him over. None of this would have happened if I'd not...I felt safe and forgot the risk Tyler could bring." I sob into my hands. Just remembering how I saw Tyler on the corner, staring at me with deadly intent, should have warranted more common sense. I put Blake into this position, and my heart's breaking because of it.

"Princess, no tears for me," Blake mutters from the gurney.

"You're awake." I lurch forward, hugging him. He grunts, and I pop back up because I'm an idiot.

"I'm so sorry."

"Don't be, princess," he groans. The man is on the edge of death, and I practically tackled him. I'm just so happy he's alive that I'm overwhelmed

"Amelia, can you call Carly so she can get a hold of our parents?"

I nod. "Of course."

He grabs my hand with his right arm, holding it tight as we ride the rest of the way to the hospital.

"Call them as soon as we get there, Mel," Felix says.

"Mel?" Blake eyes Felix. Even weakened, he's jealous. "What the hell?"

"He's one of my friends."

"Felix, this is my..." I'm about to say boyfriend, but Blake squeezes my hand and answers himself.

"I'm Blake Reynolds, Amelia's fiancé." I eyeball him, but it's not the right time to argue with him. Felix eyes us, then chuckles inwardly. "That's great. Now rest so we can get you all patched up and ready to go home."

We pull into the ER entrance. Felix helps me out before he and his partner get Blake. They rush him in and the doctors take over.

"You can't go in. Please wait here and make the calls like he asked. He's going to be fine." I'm stopped at the surgical doors.

"See you soon, Princess." He gives me a wink as they wheel him away.

"Is that fuck dead?" Blake asks Felix and the doctor wheel him away. "We can only hope so," I hear Felix say.

Now it's time to call his sister. This won't go over well. She's going to be devastated. "Carly, hi. This is Amelia."

"Of course it is. What's up, girl? I should be back in the shop before the holiday."

"It's not about that. The EMTs said he's going to be fine, but Blake was shot today."

"What! Shot! Blake! No, that can't be." Oh goodness. That didn't come out right.

"Shot!" Another woman screams in the background. I have a feeling it's his mother, but I can't be sure.

"It's in the arm. Tyler came after me and..." I break down again. Shit. This is all my fault.

"And Blake, of course, saved his woman. We'll be on our way."

"Okay," I say, sitting on the nearest chair while hoping they'll let me see him.

My dad rushes through the door seconds later, and I run into his arms. "Baby, don't cry. I'm sure he's going to be fine."

"I hope so."

After about five minutes, he sits me down. "I know this is a hard time for you, but I need to ask some questions." I forget he's the sheriff for a minute. Of course, he needs to know about the shooting. "What happened?"

"I invited Blake over for dinner. And, well, Blake was in the bathroom, and I was checking on the food when Tyler came in with a gun aimed at me. He wanted me to die. He said that if he couldn't have me that no one could. And that he was going to kill Blake too. Then Blake came up on his side and they fought. Blake was shot and then told me to hide and call the police."

"Tyler was shot as well. Did you or Blake shoot him?"

"Blake did while I was calling the police."

"Thank God. I could have lost you tonight." He wraps me in his arms, tears pouring down his face. "Damn it, Amelia. I thought losing you to him was going to be bad, but I'd take that any day to the reality that I almost lost you forever."

"I'm sorry, Dad. I should have told you sooner."

"No, I think the timing was right. He would have come after you anyway sooner or later."

"Thank you. I'm going to wash my face." I enter the bathroom, trying to contain my sadness. Thinking about Blake's mini-tirade in the ambulance gave me a little comfort.

"Amelia," Carly calls out. I turn to her and give the best fake smile I can muster.

"How did you get here so fast?"

"Doing a hundred in a seventy zone. But it's been a long time. Your dad is worried about you. He says you've been in here for about fifteen minutes. He was about to come looking for you."

"Really? I thought it was just a few. I'm sorry."

"Girl, you are losing it. When Blake called about you, I knew that it was a done deal. My brother's strong. He's going to make it."

"Thanks. Where are your parents?"

"I think they went to talk to the doctors. My mom has been tripping, but that's what it's like to be a mom," she says. Her eyes have a faraway look in them. I wonder...

Chapter Eight

Blake

I wake up to the sound of Carly snapping at someone. I open my eyes, and judging from the coat, it's one of the doctors here. "You idiot. That's my brother. Fix him or I'll..."

"You'll what, sweetheart? He's going to be fine, but you, on the other hand, should be fucking lying down and resting." My ears perk up, but the meds they gave me are making me sleepy.

"I don't need to lie down," she argues; sounds like typical Carly.

"You're carrying my kid. You'll do as I fucking say." I open my eyes, but Carly's walking out with the doctor. In comes Amelia and my sister is forgotten. God, she's beautiful even with the puffy eyes and tear-stained face.

"Amelia," I call out, though my voice is a little raspy. I hate that she's crying for me. That's something I hope never happens again. Well, except when it's my time as an old, decrepit man.

"You're awake," she says, coming to my side.

I look up at her, aching to pull her into the bed with me, but I'm sure her dad would finish the job Tyler started. "I need a kiss."

"Well, if I must kiss my brave knight," she sighs, lowering her head. I lift my good arm and wrap it around her neck and into her hair.

"I love you, Blake."

"Good. That means our date is still on."

"Yes, it is." I give her another kiss before a cough interrupts us. Amelia takes a step back, and I spot my parents.

"Blake, sweetie," my mom sobs, coming up for a hug. "Oh my goodness. When we got the call... Don't ever scare us like that again."

"I won't." She kisses my forehead before my dad takes her place.

"You took years off our lives. That means we're going to need some grandbabies pretty soon to max out on that time."

"I plan on it, Dad." Amelia blushes. I take her hand and make the introductions. "Mom, Dad, I'd like you to meet my future wife. Amelia doesn't know it yet, but I'm a stubborn man."

"Carly's already told us so much about you! I can't wait to start planning for the wedding. You need to tell me all your favorite colors and flowers. And a list of all the people you want to invite."

"Mother, let the girl breathe," Carly says, entering the room with a mask on her face. She gives me a quick hug, then turns her attention to my woman. "Hi, bro. I'm ecstatic that I picked the perfect time to get sick. Although, I wish I told the sheriff about jackass Tyler. I'm so glad he's going to rot in jail, or by the time we're done with him, at least."

"Same here. Now, who was in here earlier, little sister? I'd like to have a talk with the doctor." She blanches, and we both come to a silent understanding that I'm aware of some things she hadn't told anyone.

"Well, I'll let him know. Excuse me." I know she's finding a way to hide until later, but it's cool. I'll have to beat his ass later. If what he said was true, he knocked up my little sister.

"So, you met the hot doctor?" my mother asks.

"You know about him?" Amelia questions, giving her a smirk.

"What do you know about him, Princess?" I accuse. She never mentioned him before. "Nothing more than you do, Blake. He's stopped in the bakery several times since it opened. She likes him."

"It didn't sound that way to me," I growl.

"Well, that's not my business." She shrugs it off, but fuck if I'm not envious of the guys that got to meet Amelia before I did.

"Damn right, it's not. I don't appreciate you talking to the *hot* doctor," I tell her. Pure jealousy is eating at me. I didn't get a look at the guy, but the fact that she knows him and my mom called him hot just doesn't add up.

"Don't go getting all crazy with me yet. Save that for later down the line when I can gut punch your ass. Now get some rest. I'm going to talk to my dad." She kisses me before leaving with attitude in her step.

"Son, you know that sex and love aren't the same thing. Don't push the girl away before we have a wedding and some grandbabies."

"Mother, first—this isn't a conversation I want to have

with you. So on to the next topic...I need to rest. I have a headache."

"We'll have the nurse give you some meds," my dad tells me, smirking as he escorts my mom out. I can see visions of baby clothes in her eyes. She's been about that since Carly and I graduated college.

Chapter Nine

Amelia

It's Valentine's Day, and the bakery closed an hour early. I'm standing in the mirror, feeling beautiful. Carly's here to assist me. I'm girly, but not to the point I want to be. Carly did my makeup and helped me pick out this dress. It has a V-neck dip between my breasts that is excessively low, but I want to do all I can to drive him nuts.

Since he got out of the hospital, he's been at the bakery, sitting in the office trying to help. Carly came back yesterday feeling a hundred percent. Her flu wasn't a very dangerous one, but she's still supposed to take it easy.

Every day, he grunts and snarls at all the men that come in and flirt with me. I don't return any of it, but once they see Blake, they walk back out. He hired his guard again to follow me around so he can work without worrying while I'm at school. Afterwards, we go back to my house to hang out. Then he stays at his sister's. It's easier to keep both of us from being tempted. His arm needs to heal.

We haven't had sex since that night, but we're more than ready for it. It seems that Blake likes to tease me all day.

He passes by me, grabbing my hip and accidentally bumping me with his cock against my ass. Every night, he grinds on my butt, turning us both on. I know he's hurting too, so tonight I plan to work out that pain for him.

The doorbell rings, and I'm eager to get to him. "You look great. Go make me a niece or nephew. Mom's already planning the wedding."

"Thanks, Carly. For everything. Even getting sick."

"Anytime. Except for the sick part," she grumbles. I open the door to see Blake standing there rocking on his heels. His eyes widen and his mouth falls open.

"How am I supposed to take you out looking like that?"

"What? Is there something wrong with it?"

"Yes, and no...I mean...damn it, I can't think. All the blood's gone to my dick. Come on, Princess. I'm almost getting the strength back in my arm, and you're going to have me knocking men out tonight," he states, pulling me into his arms and kissing me. His lips feel so good on mine that I can't wait.

"Let's go, Ms. Wright." I finally notice that he's not in his truck. He has a limo, with a driver standing there holding the door open. We walk to the car and he tells the guy, "Tuck those eyes in buddy. She's mine."

"A limo?" It's my second time being in one, and the last there was like four couples for prom.

"Yes, Princess. I want you all to myself and well, since we have a long drive, I don't want to go without touching you."

"Where are you taking me?"

"You'll see."

We're driving down the main highway when the limo pulls off, and that's when I see the sign. It's a massive billboard. "Will you marry me, Princess? – Your Knight." I turn back to look at him, and he's kneeling with a ring in his hand.

"I wasn't going to ask because I already told you it was a done deal, but I want something to seal it. What do you say, Amelia? Will you marry me?"

"Yes, of course," I cry as he slides a stunning diamond ring on my finger. I can't believe this is happening. Wow. I'm trying to hold it together, but I want to celebrate with my fiancé.

"I'm going to fucking spank you if you keep crying, Princess. I don't like when you do that." I turn my ass toward him, looking for any bit of his hands on me. He looks toward the front of the limo, and the divider is in use.

He grabs the hem of my dress and slides it up. I'm wearing barely-there panties, and he growls. Blake swats my ass once, then lowers his head, kissing my stinging bottom. I'm soaked, and Blake knows it since he pushes two fingers inside me. I clench around them, nearly ready to come. He puts his hand to my mouth, stopping me from screaming.

With his whole body leaning over mine, he whispers, "You're mine. Your moans and orgasms are for me only." I can feel him use his uninjured arm to undo his pants. "Now, if you can keep it down, I'm going to fill you up. Do you want that, Princess?"

"Yes," I stutter. He easily pushes into me from behind, and I feel stretched. I turn my head toward my shoulder and use it to muffle my moan. Within a few thrusts, we're both coming. His hand goes to my mouth, and I bite down as I come. It's not hard, but it sets him off and I feel him pulse inside me.

We straighten up, him handing me some tissues that are conveniently in the limo. I rest my head on his chest, sleepy and satisfied. We arrive in Houston, and he takes me to a large building. As we get out, I feel a bit sexy knowing I have his come between my thighs. We enter, and there's a makeshift dining area set up. It's decorated completely for Valentine's Day. The thing is, it's just us two. "You arranged this?"

"Yes, the very next day after meeting you. I've been waiting for almost two weeks for your undivided attention. Now, my future Mrs. Reynolds, let's enjoy our dinner." He helps me to my seat, and as I look around the room, I don't see anyone else.

"Where are the servers?"

"As I said, my sweet princess—undivided."

I arch my brow at him after he lifts the lids off our dinner. It's the same meal I had planned the day I almost lost him. "I don't know if it'll be as good as yours smelled, but I felt like a last-minute change on the menu."

"Thank you, Blake." With every bite, I find his eyes on me. He licks his lips and groans as I let a moan slip as the meat melts in my mouth.

"Fuck. Dinner is over, Princess." He tosses his napkin on the table, then stands. I giggle for a moment. His cock stretches his pants to the brink of shredding.

The outline displays his size, and he's right—dinner is over. "I want dessert."

"I've got dessert for you," he mutters, his voice gruff with need.

"Really?" I ask, looking at him and feeling my face flush.

"Yes," he says, nodding and taking my hand. I stand and follow him. In the middle of a long, white table-clothed banquet table sits a large bowl of fat strawberries and a small chocolate fountain.

Smirking to myself, I poke my finger into the fountain,

coating my finger. I lift it to bring to my mouth, but Blake's faster. He bends his head and wraps his lips around my finger, sucking off the chocolate. It hits me straight to my core, and I clench my thighs together.

"Amelia, the chocolate tastes better than I imagined." He pulls me to him hard; my chest slams against his. "I want more."

I look up into his eyes and wink. "There's plenty of strawberries and skewers right there."

"Oh, no, I think those strawberries will do." He lifts me off my feet and sits me on the table next to the fountain. Stepping between my legs, he cups my face and crushes his mouth on mine. Thrusting my hands into his hair, I deepen our kiss. His hands move to my hips, tugging up my dress.

I pout as he pulls away from me. Shaking his head, he dips his fingers into the chocolate, then falls to his knees. He starts to paint my pussy lips with chocolate. The warm liquid is met by his cool breath before I feel the flick of his tongue. I toss my head back and grasp the edge of the table. I'm panting out my need. "Don't stop."

Every inch of me is so turned on that I'm going to come. He stands up, undoes his pants, and pulls out his thick, hard cock. I want to taste him, but I want him in me right now.

"We're coming together," he growled. "And I'm coming inside of you." He decides for me, pushing inside me in one long motion. I'm feeling stretched, but I want more. I rock my hips forward. He grabs the back of my head and pulls my face to his, kissing me like it's the last time. He slashes his tongue across mine, letting me taste a chocolatey version of me. I want more.

I reach over and dip my fingers into the chocolate, slipping my hands between my breasts. Giving him access, he bends his head and runs his tongue over my breasts, licking every drop of chocolate off.

I shiver and clench up, my orgasm on the cusp. Then he drives hard into me and I'm done, my body losing all the control I thought I had. For a split second, I believed I had him worked up more than me, but I was wrong. I come on his cock, squeezing him. He places his hands on the table, pinning me in, then he pumps forward, fucking me until I'm about to come again. I can't take anymore before I cry out, "I'm coming."

"That's what I want to hear—over and over again." He grunts and fills me up, coming hard, resting his head in the crook of my neck. I can feel his breath on my skin and want this moment to last forever.

"I'll give you forever." Oops, I said that aloud.

"I'm going to hold you to it."

"That's fine. As long as I get to hold you. And maybe we should invest in chocolate. I've got a new favorite sweet treat."

Blake

We got married three months after we met, and I haven't looked back. My wife is so perfect. She finished her degree in web design and now works for the family company as our site manager. She's amazing and carrying our second baby. It's time to celebrate. Just yesterday, Tyler Wills was sentenced to twenty-five years.

"Morning, Blake," Carly says, waddling her large belly around the kitchen.

"Morning, sis. Should you be in the kitchen still? You're a walking hazard," I tease, but at the same time, I'm serious. She's likely to hurt herself.

"Shut it. I'm just fine. Your wife is out helping Tracy with the customers." She knew that would get rid of me.

"Thanks. You look beautiful, by the way." I kiss her cheek, then hunt down my wife. She's smiling at some man who's clearly returning it. I'm about to do something dumb.

"Thank you, ma'am. Are you sure there's nothing in these cookies?" He smirks at her.

"I'm sure." They both begin to laugh, and I'm ready to clock him in the face. I've seen him around. He's a local cowboy with a big ranch in the next town over.

"Is there something I can help you with?" I ask, letting him know that flirting with my wife is about to get his ass dropped. I walk up to Amelia and slide my arm around her waist.

"Now I know what the secret ingredient is," he mutters.

"Oh, yeah?" Tracy asks.

"Yes—possessive husbands that love their wives."

"Take care, and the offer is open at any time." He winks and walks out.

"What the hell was that all about?" I spin her to me and kiss her hard. As soon as we stop, she giggles.

"He thinks there's some pregnancy magic in the cookies," she answers, looking down at her belly.

"Because you're all knocked up?" Even the new employee, Courtney, is pregnant.

"Yes, and so is his wife and two sisters-in-law." I have to laugh as well. He's right. Loving your wife means they give you tons of babies. Chloe is our little girl due in three months. Our son, George, was born a little over nine months after we met.

"Amelia, it's time for our date."

"I'm sorry. I lost track of time."

"I'm sure. When you ladies get started...I don't know how you all get anything done." I wave everyone off and head over to say goodbye to Carly. We get to the car, and I help her in.

"We're efficient."

"That you are," I say, kissing her lips. I want her this instant. Maybe I should have gotten a limo for tonight.

"Was George upset that you left?"

"Yes, but I promised him that Mommy would call and sing him a lullaby. He loves you so much."

"I love my little man. And I love you, Blake."

"I love you, too," I whisper, bringing her hand to my lips and kissing her soft skin. "Mm...chocolate."

"I have a special treat for you." She pulls out a small piping bag with chocolate in it. I start laughing. "Damn, Princess, you know I like your pussy, but add a little chocolate and I'm going to orgasm you to sleep." I never realized I had a sweet tooth until I met Amelia.

She lifts it up, tips her head back, then squeezes a small dab into her mouth. Pressing her lips together, she moans, then licks them. The visual is getting me hard as fuck. I'm going to give her something to moan about.

I grunt, trying to hang in until we get to our house. The short drive seems to take forever. We pull into the garage. I let the door close and carry her into the house.

Three hours, a handful of orgasms, and a whole bag of chocolate later, we're passing out.

"Happy Valentine's Day, my knight."

"Happy Valentine's Day, my princess."

Doctor's Orders, Sweetheart

Introduction

Carly: Have you ever met someone you want to kick in the shins and kiss at the same time?

Well, Carter James is that kind of guy for me. He's a hot pediatric doctor with a heart of gold for his patients and insanely tempting eye candy for the moms trolling the children's ward. He's cocky and treats me like one of the children.

Carter: Have you ever met the one for you, but they think you're a total jerk?

Carly Reynolds is that kind of woman for me. She's a hot volunteer that drives me crazy. I want her in every way, so much so I can't stop looking out for her well-being. She's going to push me over the edge one day, and I'm going to claim what I've wanted for six months—her.

Carly

Standing outside, I stare at my new bakery in total amazement. The sun rests on the horizon waiting to rise, yet I can still tell my sign is perfect. I'll have to thank my brother, Blake, for his excellent work on it. Sweetheart's Treats is mine, and it's surreal that I'm about to open in a few hours.

Even though I'm in the middle of Texas, it's January and the chill hits me hard, so it's time to head inside before I freeze in my little sweater. The key turns effortlessly in the lock, and I step into the building my parents helped me purchase.

I'm not ashamed to admit that I had a hand up from them. They are the most amazingly kind and loving parents anyone could ask for, and I hope to be like them when I finally marry and have a family. After graduating from culinary school with a certification in pastries, I couldn't wait to start my own business. I should have started as a baker for someone else, but my parents have complete faith in me.

I'm going to need an employee or two, but for the time

being, I have to start baking. My ingredients are waiting for me, which means all I need to do is get my apron and put my curly blonde hair into a perfect bun before I can begin.

Within minutes, I smell the fresh scents of sugar and chocolate in the air. It brings me to a time when I used to visit my grandmother and we would spend hours baking. More like I would end up with flour everywhere and she would pull out fresh-baked pies and cupcakes. Those days are gone, but I'll never forget everything she taught me.

This is a small town with no other bakery, so I'm certain they'll come flocking here once I gain some foot traffic. My family owns a large printing and signage company and prepared all my marketing materials with my input.

The town had a bakery a long time ago, but the family sold the building once the owner died. It's been at least ten years, and it's time they had fresh-baked goods again instead of the pre-packaged stuff from the major grocery store in town. I hope they agree.

The grand opening is next week, but the soft one is today. I plan to make pastries of all sorts to gauge the needs and wants of customers. I know it's the basics that'll sell, but testing the waters is all I can do.

Coming from Houston, I thought this would be the perfect market to open in. There are tons of bakeries and stores that make fresh-baked goods, so I searched the region for a city that didn't. Palace, Texas feels like the perfect place.

After a smooth early morning of baking, decorating, and setting up, I turn the sign hanging on the door to "Open," and within a couple of minutes three women enter, shaking off the chill before meeting my gaze.

"Good morning, ladies. Welcome to Sweetheart's Treats," I say, turning on my best sweet smile even though

I'm feeling nauseous. My nerves have picked up and the show has started.

"Wow, it smells amazing in here," a woman with straight white hair that reaches her shoulders exclaims. They all smile at me. "Hello, Ms...?"

"I'm Carly Reynolds," I answer.

"Are you married?" she asks outright.

I smirk. She wastes no time, I see. "No, I'm not."

"I have a son." I bet she does. Mothers are all alike. It's something I always get from my mother's friends.

"We all know you have a son, Laura. He's handsome and a doctor. Would you leave the poor man alone?" the woman with curly salt-and-pepper hair tells her. She looks at me with a smile. I'm doing my best not to laugh out loud. "That's nothing to say about you. You are stunningly beautiful, my dear. She just won't let her son breathe."

"I understand. My mother wants grandchildren already. And my brother's being harangued daily." Blake runs from my mother any chance he gets. If not, she'll be introducing him to the next state beauty of Texas. I didn't even know they had that many pageants, and I've lived in Houston my whole life.

"I'm Greta Simms. I only have daughters, so I'll leave you be. Now—we came for a treat." She rubs her hands together like she's been waiting for this day all along. That's the passion I want to see from my customers when they're leaving the shop, and itching to return.

"I've set up a tray with free samples of this morning's treats. Please feel free to try them." The ladies take me up on my offer, and each one chooses a different kind of treat. Greta takes the strawberry scone and moans like she needs a moment alone. The other two hit the chocolate treats, but the same sound leaves their mouths.

"Girl, you are a blessing. Are you planning to do specialty orders?" Laura asks, stealing a sample of the scone.

"Yes, but it will be minimal for the time being. I don't have any employees yet."

"Well, I'd like a dozen of these to drop off to my son. He loves strawberries, and I know he'd enjoy these. He works in Pediatrics at St. Joseph's Regional Medical Center." I hold back a gasp because I probably know who he is. Studying her face, I'm sure it's the man I despise and lust over with the same thought.

"I actually volunteer in the children's wing on Sundays," I admit. The world is truly small. They say Texas is huge, but I'm calling bullshit. I can't escape Carter. He's everywhere, especially in my thoughts.

"So you've met my son," she gushes.

"I don't know all the doctors there." I truly don't. Not everyone works on Sundays, and I've only been going for six months.

"He's Dr. Carter James." And he's the only doctor I've managed to run into every time I visit. The tall, sexy man with the wickedly promising smile destroys my beauty sleep and peace of mind.

What amuses me is that she thinks she needs to find him a woman. He is a freaking hottie, and every single nurse wants to be with him. Several mothers in the ward smile at him like they're looking for a stepdad for their children. Seriously, the man's extremely handsome and smart. Who wouldn't want someone like that? Well, except me.

"Oh, yes, I've met Dr. James. He's a nice man. The kids and the mothers love him," I remark with as much sweetness as I can muster.

Carter and I have a tumultuous relationship. More like he tries to goad me, and I avoid him as if he has the plague.

He keeps picking on me, constantly treating me like one of the children in the ward—helpless and vulnerable—and I want to deck him.

He even tied my shoes one day. What grown-ass man does that? I'm an adult, but I guess since I'm not a doctor, I'm not smart enough to function on my own.

"He needs to get married before I kick the bucket, but he's too busy, or so he claims." Not on Sundays. Every time I turn around, my four-hour visit is plagued with his presence. And, he likes to keep tabs on me as if I'm going to accidentally kill one of the kids.

"We've got to go, so can we please get some treats?" Greta asks, eyeing the brownies. I forget about Carter for half a second as I show her the brownies. The overwhelming pleasure I get from people enjoying my products helps me cope with my insane feelings for the jackass.

Laura joins us at the display case. "Sorry—I can't help myself. My son's wonderful, and I want him to be happy." The genuine humility she displays tells me she loves him so much.

Greta reprimands her. "Then leave the boy alone. I'll take two brownies and three of the peanut butter cookies."

"I thought you didn't like peanut butter cookies?" the other woman with red and gray hair questioned.

"I don't, but the hubby does. The brownies are for me."

Boxing up their treats, I'm pleased to see them off. I couldn't take much more of her mentioning Carter. I had a crush on him when we first met. After one day in his presence, I regretted it.

The way he makes my heart thump is irrational. I want to jump into his arms and kiss him silent while at the same time gut-punching him. Damn, the man drives me bananas.

Chapter Two

Carter

"Darling," I hear, turning to see the person I know the voice belongs to. My mother smiles charmingly. She's definitely who I get it from.

"Hello, Mother. What brings you to see me?" I ask, looking at her suspiciously. She only comes when she wants to know if there's anyone new in my life. I haven't had a date in years, and yet she doesn't give up. I'm not going to tell her about the insane obsession with a woman who hates me.

"Can't I come bring you a delicious snack?" she exclaims, giving me a pouty look. I twist my lips, not buying her fake indignation.

"You brought me a snack?" She uses every excuse, but this is a new one. I don't eat sweets since I try to keep in shape. There's only one sweet thing I want to eat, but she runs from me at every turn.

I take the box and see a label on the top. It's Sweetheart's Treats Bakery. I've never heard of the place, but considering I don't eat goodies, that could be one reason.

Then I notice the fine print: *1001 Main Street, Palace, Texas*.

"Where's Palace, Texas, and why did you go there? Surely there's a bakery nearby," I say as I open the box. Wow, my mouth is watering just from the smell. I close the box because I'm tempted to eat them. As good as they are, I'll save them for the nursing staff, who work hard.

"Gosh, can't I just do something nice for you?" This time, I've really offended her. Immediately, I feel like a dick. She just wants the best for me, but I'm a man and can decide that for myself.

"Sorry, Mom. Thanks for these. They smell fantastic." I give her a kiss on the cheek. She knows how much I love strawberries, but I prefer fresh ones.

"Aww, that's so sweet," Ivy, one of the head nurses, mocks as she comes up.

"Don't you have work to do?" I mutter, trying to rankle her because she gets on my nerves lately. She knows I'm interested in Carly and teases me about it.

"Yes, and so do you," she chides, handing me a chart while snatching the box from my hands. She's right—I do. She looks down at the box and shakes her head. I'm about to walk away when I hear her squeal, "Oh my God! You went to Carly's bakery."

I freeze, halting all movement except my insanely out-of-control heart. I turn around and ask, "Carly who?" Tell me it's not my Carly she's talking about.

"The one that comes every week that you scare off," she remarks, jutting her chin out.

I snatch the box back. "These are mine. I'll put them in my office." Both ladies giggle, and I turn a hard glare their way. My mom knows all about my Carly, sneaky woman.

Knowing Carly made them makes me want to eat them

all. I take a deep breath and set the box on my desk. I can't believe she opened a bakery. I never heard about it. Then again, she refuses to talk to me unless it's necessary.

I'm not sure what I did wrong for her to hate me. Every other woman with a pulse can't stop following me around and hangs on my every word, despite me showing them no damn interest. However, the one I've wanted from the first time I saw her—brushing the hair of a girl who broke her leg—hates me. I've been hooked on Carly, and nothing and no one can shake my addiction.

I make it through the day, hoping time would fly. Checking Google Maps, I plan my path to see Carly. I'm off in two days, and then I'll make a trip to Palace. The longing to see her continues to build as I watch the clock. Since she's a volunteer, I only get to see her once a week. I don't know where she lives, and Human Resources won't give me that information. I've considered hiring a private investigator; I didn't realize I had one in my mother.

As soon as I get to my condo, I call my mother. "Hello, Carter, darling. How are you?" She's overly cheerful, and I'm wondering if she's been drinking wine early today.

"I'm great, but a little confused. How did you find out about Carly's bakery?"

"Oh, Carter, you have way too many snitches in your midst. You know I'm friends with some of the hospital staff. They told me about your bad attitude to the little beauty. And now I know why. She's perfect, Carter, and truly a sweetheart. No wonder you call her that."

"I only do it to aggravate her," I lie. It's because that's the way I see her. I fell in love with her kind and sweet heart. It didn't help that she's fucking sexy as hell. Everything wonderful in a little package.

"Don't lie to me. I'm your mother," she challenges.

"Mother, please stay out of it. But thank you for telling me where to find her."

"Of course, darling. Happy hunting, son." I roll my eyes because she's relentless.

"I'm working tomorrow for twelve hours. Please just let it go. I'll do what I can, but if she doesn't want anything to do with me, then there's nothing more I can do."

"Work harder on pleasing the woman, not pissing her off. That's a good start." I don't know why I piss her off. I'm constantly worried about her and doing things to help her. Well, in two days I'm going to visit her, and she'll learn she's mine.

Chapter Three

Carly

"Amelia, I'm so glad you came to work for me. I had no idea how crazy it was going to be yesterday," I say as we take out the first trays. We've been working for three hours to get everything ready.

"This is just what I needed," she replies, twisting the lock on the front door and opening it to the line of customers waiting.

"Good morning, ladies," the local sheriff greets us. He's a handsome man.

"Hello, Sheriff," I say. We haven't met formally, but someone mentioned him yesterday in passing. Since the town is so small, he and two deputies are enough to handle it. I'm so used to cops patrolling everywhere that it's kind of nice.

"Hi, Dad. What brings you to see me?" *Dad*? He looks way too young. Wow. Well, his wife is a lucky woman.

"I came to see how it's going. You left your old job like a hot pot." Her dad is on to her. I doubt she's going to tell him, though.

"This one is already better. Besides, it's closer to the house and no late nights."

"Yes, that's right. Let me know if you need anything. I've got to go. Ms. Reynolds, it's a pleasure to meet you. Hopefully, you can come over for dinner one day," he says, tipping his hat before walking out.

"Wow, your dad is young and hot."

"I suppose so. It was an accidental teen pregnancy thing, and my mom didn't want that life. She left when I was little."

"Oh, well, that sucks. I'm sorry."

"Don't be. It worked out for the best. My dad is pretty wonderful."

"He seems like it." The timer goes off in the kitchen. "I'll be back."

For some reason, I can't get Carter out of my head. I wonder if he liked the scones. Did he know I made them? Goodness, the man thought so damn little of me, and here I am panting over him. Sleep has eluded me the past two nights because of him.

I set the cookies to cool after taking them out, then start icing the cupcakes. It takes me ten minutes to finish the next batch, and I hear people coming and going. I step into the storefront with them, aiming to lend a hand.

A gasp falls from my lips when I see none other than Carter James. He's standing there in a hoodie and pair of jeans that hug his ass so damn perfectly. I hate the man and the way he makes me feel. A sudden surge of jealousy pumps through me as I see him smiling at Amelia—just like he does everyone, and they all eat it up.

They turn when they hear me come out. Amelia smiles wildly at me, tilting her head toward Dr. Hottie. He's got his eyes glued to mine. His brown hair looks thoroughly ran through. When my time at the hospital starts every week, it's always perfectly smoothed back, but by the end of the day, it looks like this. It makes me wonder if he fucks nurses or horny moms in his office. I'm immediately repulsed, which helps deal with seeing him.

"Hello, Dr. James," I snidely say, carrying the tray to the counter. As I make my way, he steps up and takes it from me.

"It's Carter, Carly," he whispers, setting it on the counter. His athletic frame moves closer to me like a tiger smoothly stalking his prey, staring at me with a cocky smirk. My heart's racing, which infuriates me even more. How dare he come here. "I know your name. I'm just wondering what you're doing here."

"I came to get more scones. They were delicious." God, I must be crazy, or I just really need to get off because it sounded like he wasn't talking about scones.

"Did you share, or eat them all yourself?" I ask, wondering if he gave them to his groupies at the hospital.

"He doesn't seem like he eats goodies, Carly," Amelia remarks, and I want to kick her ass for looking at him. I throw a fierce scowl her way. She tosses her hands up and goes back to putting away the cupcakes.

He smiles at me and then says, "Not normally, but these were the best treat ever."

"You drove all the way here for scones?" I snipe. My brain is completely confused. I want him to stay, and also to go. It's truly infuriating the way he seems pleased with himself for making the journey. "Well, we're all out. Sorry. Is there something else I can get you?"

"How about you bring them Sunday?"

"I will. How many do you want?" I ask, trying to maintain a level of indifference. He came here for treats to give his women. I've never seen him with anyone, but then again, at work he's the consummate professional. *Asshole.*

"A dozen just for me, and another two for the hospital. Here's my credit card. Just bring it back then, sweetheart." He winks after setting it down on the counter, then waves at Amelia before walking out. I'm so stunned that I'm at a loss for what just happened. He drove all this way for something and then left. What the fuck? He gave me his card. What the hell is he trying to prove? That he can buy his own treats? Did he not like looking like a mama's boy?

"Damn, I thought he was going to kiss you."

"What? The man thinks I'm incompetent."

"Whoa, girl, please. He didn't drive all the way from Houston to stop for two minutes. He asked where you were and said his nosy mother had been in here."

"Whatever. There's plenty of work to do." I wave her off and take his card into my office, tucking it into my purse so I don't lose it. I'd hate for him to get on me about not being able to handle one credit card.

Chapter Four

Carter

It's Sunday, and I'm waiting for her to come in. I'm snapping at everyone in my way because I'm in a constant state of sexual frustration. It's not just the lust driving me. I want to hold Carly and tell her that I want her to have my babies.

She fucks up my sense of right and wrong. I ache to take her hard and fast in my office and fill her up. Or fuck—the nearest bed will do.

I'm officially nuts when it comes to her. I play back my behavior when I went into her shop. What the fuck did I do? I feel like a total asshole. Instead of trying to talk to her, convince her to want me, I made a fool of myself. I never stammer over my words with anyone I speak with.

For six months I've been watching her, loving the way she smiles and laughs. She gives joy to everyone around her. Damn, she's so perfect for me, and I want her for myself.

I really hadn't planned on buying any of her goodies for the hospital. Selfishly, I don't want to share Carly's treats with anyone. They should all be for me. Everything about Carly should be for me.

Fuck, that mouth of hers belongs to me as well. I might lose control and kiss her today. I need to be careful and wait until she begs for it. It's not that I want her to take the lead, but I could lose my job if I don't. I want her affection, but all I do is make her mad.

It's time for her to come in, and when she does, I go to my office like I've forgotten she was coming. As the director of the children's wing, I have my own for meetings and the like.

All directors in the building do, but the rest of the doctors use a large office on each floor. I wrap myself up in my work, hoping that I make it through the day without acting like an ass.

About ten minutes after her arrival, she knocks on my open office door.

"Dr. James, I'm here with your treats." I can't stand because my dick is instantly hard. Her long blonde hair is in a braid that she has thrown over her right shoulder. She's in her typical bright colors because one of the kids here for the foreseeable future loves it. Her top is tight enough to hug her large tits but still appropriate to be around small kids. If I get up, she'll see how pleased I am to see her.

Fuck, I'm ready to bend her over my desk and rut my kids into her. She's a true ray of sunshine, and I want to kiss the fuck out of her and take in all her light. Damn, the woman makes me feel poetic. I haven't written a poem since I was in eighth grade, and I had to.

Still, I can only manage a grunt before saying, "Leave them on the table." She sets them on the small round table we use for meetings, and a new picture plays in my mind. I could see her splayed out on her back with my face between her thighs, having my own treat. Fuck. I wonder if she's as sweet as she looks.

"Fine. Here's your card and receipt," she says, dropping them on my desk, then spinning on her heels and leaving my office, slamming the door. Damn it. I bang my head on my desk onto an open Physician's Desk Reference, softening the blow. I want to kick my own ass. My stupid cock can't handle being around her. It's a big reason why I only steal short moments in her presence.

As soon as my dick calms down, I walk out of my office, taking the boxes with me. I don't see her when I go into the breakroom, but I drop off the scones anyway.

Then I head over to the children's playroom. There she is, sitting on the floor with several kids, reading a story. I have to find a way to win her. Once I learn to stop being tense and overprotective around her, I can get her to see the real me.

Ivy calls me into the ER where they need a pediatric physician. I head down, regretting I didn't get to apologize. I spend the next four hours in the ER and once I get back, she's gone for the day and won't return until next week. I look at my schedule and see that I'm off next Sunday, but by the end of the day, I've switched schedules and now I'm off on Friday instead. This way I can see my woman again. I plan to stop by her shop on Friday and ask her out.

Friday comes, but my mom needs me to fix a few things around the house. After I'm done, I drive to the bakery. "Where's the boss lady?"

"She's at the hospital. She changed her day to today."

"Oh. Well, excuse me." I lightly tap the counter and

walk out of the bakery as a deep ache fills my chest. Hell, I think my heart just fucking broke.

I drive back to my condo and fall asleep. There's nothing I can do, and since I promised to rearrange my schedule, I won't be seeing her.

Maybe it's what I need.

Chapter Five

Carly

I haven't seen Carter in two weeks. The little boy I work with, Simon, had to change his therapy times, so I did the same thing. I had no idea that meant I wouldn't see Carter. I missed him more than humanly possible. My heart hurts, but he made it clear that Amelia's claims were way off base. He hasn't shown up since, and it feels god-awful. I thought I wouldn't miss him, but I was wrong.

It's Friday, and several kids are playing so I join them. I've been visiting for about an hour when Carter comes running into the room. "Carly, you're not supposed to be in here. Out, now," he barks out. I look at him like he's fucking crazy. I stand and get in his face.

"What's your problem?" I spit out through gritted teeth so the kids don't hear me. They are playing with their toys and coloring, ignoring us.

"You are fucking going to get sick," he roars, grabbing me by my elbow and directing me to his office. It's a little rough, but I want more of it. I bite back a moan. My panties are soaked.

"What the hell do you care?" I challenge him. He's been nothing but mean to me, and now he's essentially dragging me away from the only joy I get out of coming here. Closing his office door, his arms bracket me in, my back against the door.

"What do I care? I worry about you all the goddamn time. I do everything I can to make sure nothing happens to you, and yet you do your best to drive me insane," he growls out, and before I know what's happening, his mouth is on mine.

I moan, my hands gripping his collar, pulling him down harder. I try crawling up his body, throwing my legs around his waist. He cups my ass and drags his cock along the edge of my pussy. I clench every time his ridge rubs my clit.

I'm so glad I wore a skirt today. It's warm enough for it, and a part of me hoped he'd be here.

"I can't stop thinking about you, Carly," he confesses.

"I've missed you, Carter," I pant between kisses. I need more. I crave more.

"I'm off for the rest of the day. Let's go now because I have to be back tomorrow." I agree and follow along even though I shouldn't. I can't believe what we're about to do, but if he'd stripped me bare in his office, I would have given it up to him. We take his SUV to his condo. The entire drive he's holding my hand, placing tiny kisses on it as we make our way through the busy streets.

We drive into an underground parking lot, and he pulls into a personalized spot next to the elevators. "Wait here," he orders before hopping out. He rushes around and opens the door, pulling me into his arms and carrying me out.

"I can walk."

"I know, but I've longed for this. I need to care for you, sweetheart." He slams his mouth on mine. I don't see a thing because we can't stop kissing during the elevator ride and into his place. He carries me into the bedroom, and I'm on the verge of coming on the spot. At twenty-one, I'm no innocent girl, but I've never gone all the way with anyone. Carter is all man, and I know he'll give me all I need.

"You're going to come hard and fast for me. Then, I'm going to fuck you until you scream again." He grabs the hem of my top, lifting it over my head. He flings it behind him, biting his lip and staring at my breasts. I'm so glad I wore the sexiest bra I own.

"Damn, I'm going to do what I can to hold on, but you've got me so hard." He grabs the bra and literally rips it off me. "I'll buy you a new one," he says after I gasp. He pushes me onto the bed, then bends down to slip off my heels before pulling down my skirt. I squeal and giggle as his mouth kisses my inner thigh. His stubble rubs along my skin, and I want more. My hands clench the sheets as he presses his face into my covered pussy. The feel of his warm breath sends shivers down my body. He growls, tearing my panties completely off, then slams his tongue into my core. I'm spread out on the bed with my legs on either side of his face. Every ounce of pleasure simmers inside me, and I know I'm about to come for him.

"Mine," he grunts against my pussy. He looks at me, then softly bites my clit. I explode. He slides his shirt off, revealing a killer set of abs, and my pussy clenches again. "Damn, sweetheart. You're pussy tastes so damn sweet." He drops back down on his knees while working his pants off, and his mouth hits my clit again. I'm on the verge of coming a second time. I need to feel him inside me.

"I need you, Carter. Please fuck me," I cry out, arching my back off the bed as he hits my sweet spot. He bites my thigh before sliding into me. God, I'm being stretched to the max, and then he freezes.

He looks down at me, then takes my hands and lifts them above my head. "You're all mine. Relax—this will only hurt for a second." I can't because I need him to take me. In one long stroke, he takes my virginity. A tear escapes, and he looks like I've stabbed him in the heart.

"I didn't mean to hurt you, Carly," he whispers, bending down and kissing it away. I fall into his kiss, and my pussy tightens around his large cock. I love the way his strong body is holding mine down. "I need you to come for me. Can you do that for me, sweetheart?"

"Anything for you," I moan, tugging my hands out of his. He smiles when I wrap one around his neck and into his hair.

"Keep it up, and you'll be wrapped in these sheets forever," he murmurs into my ear before rocking back and forth. His thick cock slides out and back in completely, slamming into my womb. I'm coming and let him know. My hands claw down his back with my hips thrusting up. "That's it, Carly. Come for me." He reaches between us and presses his thumb on my clit. I come harder and feel him join me.

Chapter Six

Carter

I can't believe this. In my bed, in my arms, is the only woman I want to be with. The one who hated me. I roll over and take her with me, keeping my dick deep inside her. I want every drop of cum to stay within her so my baby will grow in her womb. Sealing her to me would be a joy I couldn't even express. It's underhanded as fuck, but I don't care because I'd do anything to make Carly mine forever.

"What time do you have to go to work?" she asks.

"Four am," I mutter, rubbing her back. She attempts to sit up, but I hold her to me even though sadly I'm no longer inside her. My cock stiffens every time she moves.

"Perfect. I need to get to the bakery by six at the latest," she says like there's nothing going on but a casual hookup.

"Carly, are you going to pretend this isn't happening?" I ask her, wanting to get into that complex head of hers.

She looks down at me, "No, but I don't understand it, Carter. You treat me like a child, and yes, I'm a lot younger than you and I'm not a doctor, but I'm old enough to own a business." She attempts to get away from me again, but this time, I flip her onto her back and pin her down to the mattress.

Running the back of my hand down her cheek, I respond to her tirade. "I don't mean to. Hell, I'd never consider you like that at all. I find you to be the most beautiful, kind, and caring woman. I was just looking out for you."

"So what was today about? You yelled at me." Her brow raises so prettily, but I brush it down with my thumb.Leaning in a steal a peck. She tries to move away, but I kiss her anyway. "Don't try to distract me, Dr. James."

"I'm sorry, you just looked so adorable." She frowns, and I suppose adorable doesn't help my cause. "Anyway, I panicked when I saw you in there. They all have Influenza B. I don't want you to get it."

"Oh, no one said anything. Okay, I get your concern, but you didn't have to be so mean." She pushes on my chest and I let her up only to lean against the headboard and drag her onto my lap.

"Sweetheart, they weren't supposed to let you in there. I need to write someone up. Whoever gave you clearance didn't tell you it wasn't safe. Which reminds me—why did you change your schedule on me?"

"I didn't do it to avoid you. One of the boys changed his time to come for treatments, and I couldn't break his heart by missing our visit."

"I guess I could forgive you for it, but if you came when you were supposed to come, then you wouldn't have been exposed to the kids with the flu."

"I never get sick, Carter. I'll be fine."

"Don't argue with me. I'm always going to worry about you. If something hurts you, then it destroys me," I tell her, brushing my hands over her hair.

"Then what happened in your office?" She stares at me, and I see the hurt. "You didn't care about my feelings then."

I shake my head. "Sweetheart, I was stiff as fuck and ready to pound you against my desk until you were screaming my name," I admit, rubbing my hands over her back.

"Like you are right now," she purrs, straddling my thighs and rocking back and forth, taking my cock inside her. Her hands press onto my chest as she works her pussy on me. I help her get fully seated on my dick. "Round two," she adds, rolling her hips, and the pleasure shoots through me. Her hair bounces in time with her perfect tits as she rides me. I play with her hard peaks, plucking on them, squeezing her breasts. I lean forward and suck on one, then move to the other. Fuck. I nip and lick my way to her throat, then crush my mouth to hers. Our tongues and lips meet, brushing and tasting each other. I yearn for more of her. This is what I want for the rest of our lives.

"Fuck. Ride me, sweetheart."

The feel of being deep inside her is indescribable. Our bodies are meant to be together. I knew she was perfect for me from the first time we met. My hands roam over her bare flesh, feeling her body burn with desire. It doesn't take long for our releases to hit and I'm filling her with my baby. I don't want anything between us, ever.

"You're mine, Carly. Now rest."

"Bossy much?"

"You better get used to it," I warn, leaning up and sucking on her nipple, then letting it pop from my mouth. I rest back on the pillows, pulling her onto my chest.

Chapter Seven

Carly

I hate having to part ways, but we've both got shit to do. The bakery needs to be opened, and he's got to treat some amazingly special children. We say our goodbyes outside the hospital, kissing several times before finally pulling apart. He waits for me to drive away, and through my rearview mirror, I see him go inside.

I call Amelia as I get closer to the bakery; she's probably about to head out to the shop as we speak. "Hey, Carly. How's it going?"

"I'm on my way to the shop early."

"Good, because I'll be there in ten minutes." I pull into the back and open the front door. I'm hit with an overwhelming feeling of anxiety. I have to say that it must be what happened between Carter and me. He's in my thoughts as I knead the dough for the croissants and we set up for the day. I receive a text from him about seven, but I can't check it because my hands are filled with flour and dough. It takes another twenty minutes before I can look at them.

Carter: *I miss you, sweetheart.*

Carter: *Hope you made it back safely.*

Carter: *Come on, Carly. Please respond. You're freaking me out.*

Me: *I'm fine. Sorry, hands full of flour and in the middle of baking. Not trying to bake my phone with the bread.*

Carter: *Sorry, scared me for a minute. A huge crash on the 40.*

Me: *That's terrible. I hope everyone will make it.*

Carter: *So far so good. Only one child with minor injuries. Be safe—doctor's orders.*

Me: *Yes, sir. Get to work.*

I take the next tray into the storefront, and there's the jackass who's been messing with Amelia. He just won't take no for an answer. I have a gun in my drawer, and I'll shoot the fucker if necessary. I'm from Texas, after all.

"Are you buying anything? If not, get the fuck out. I've got a brother and a Magnum that can help you decide."

"Sorry. See you later, baby," he tells Amelia. The creepy way he looks at her bothers me.

"Girl, are you okay?" I ask as soon as he's out of sight.

"Yes. He just doesn't get it. I don't want shit to do with him," she exclaims, clenching her fists in frustration. I can see that ass is on her last nerve.

"Well, if he comes around again, I'm calling the police. That POS needs to learn the hard way that I'm a great shot and will protect my friends. I dare him to come back."

"Wow, I've never seen you all 'rawr,'" she confesses, pretending to claw towards me. I laugh it off because the only one who gets to see me like that is Carter and my brother, Blake. They are the only ones to try my nerves.

This bastard did more than that and made me itch to pull out my pretty gun and put a bullet in his ass.

The timer goes off, and I shake away the frustration. "How about you get the goodies and I man the front?"

"You're the boss. Don't want to get on your bad side." She laughs, playing like she's scared of me. I roll my eyes and put away the treats. My phone buzzes, and this time my hands are clutter free.

"Hey, Mom, how's it going?"

"It's wonderful. I miss you. Can you come over tonight?"

"I can't," I answer quickly without thinking. I was going to tell her that I had a date. Just as I am about to, the phone buzzes. It's a text from Carter. *I'm pulling a double. It's a madhouse here.*

"Actually, Mom, never mind. I can make it."

"Great. I can't wait to see you. Blake's coming too."

"Good. I haven't seen him since I opened."

I end the call and go back to work, forgetting about messaging Carter back.

My phone rings ten minutes later. "Hello," I answer. I know it's Carter, but I'm not acting like a love-sick puppy even though I feel like one.

"You didn't message me back. I feel like a dick for having to cancel dinner tonight."

"It's fine. I'm going to my parents' house instead."

"Oh."

"What's wrong?"

"Nothing. I just thought you'd be upset, but you're okay with the change of plans."

"You want me upset?" I know that's not what he meant. I'm acting like I couldn't care less, but in truth, my chest hurts. It aches knowing it's going to be a long time before we see each other again.

"No, but I am. I fucking miss you like crazy, Carly."

"Carter, I miss you too. I was hurt when I got your message, but what can I do? You're a doctor, the head of the Pediatric department. It sucks, but I understand."

"I can't wait to see you. I'm off and not on call for the next two days."

"Perfect. We can spend the day together, and then you can drive to the shop with me. If you'd like, of course."

"I want to spend every moment with you, Carly. I've got to go, but, woman, take care of yourself."

I'm at my parents' a few hours later, but I feel like death warmed over me. My heart is pounding, I'm vomiting, and I'm covered in sweat. My phone buzzes, and I go to check it because I know it's got to be Carter, but I drop it in the toilet. Damn it. I reach for it because even though it's essentially a funky paperweight, I can't flush it. Taking it out sends me into another vomiting fit. I come out of the bathroom, and my brother catches me as I get dizzy. My mom goes into Dr. Mom mode as Blake carries me to my old bedroom.

"Shit," I grumble. "Get away from me. I'm contagious. I think I've got the flu."

"Damn it. Are you serious, Carly?"

"Yes. Several kids at the hospital had it, and they didn't tell me until it was too late."

"I've gotten my shots, Blake, but please go Lysol everything you can. Open the windows," I hear our mom tell him.

"Yes, Mom."

"Mom, I'll be fine," I slur.

Chapter Eight

Carter

I'm fucking freaking out. I messaged Carly last night but didn't get a response. It was pretty early, so I thought she would have texted me back. Then her phone kept going to voicemail. I don't have her family information, so I have no idea where they live or how to get in contact with them.

I go home and wait. We were perfectly fine the last time we spoke. I hope she calls me soon. I can barely sleep because I know something's wrong. It's about eleven when I get a call from the hospital.

"Ivy, what's going on?"

"Carter, I thought you should know that Carly's in the hospital. She tested positive for the flu. She came in around one this morning."

"I'm on my way. Thank you, Ivy."

"No problem. She woke up and asked if someone could get a hold of you. Something about her phone breaking. It's hard to understand her." I end the call with another thank you, dressing in record time.

I'm out of the condo and on my way to her side. Fuck, I

can't believe she's sick. My heart's thundering in my chest. As soon as I get there, I park in my spot and rush inside. I ask for her room at the security desk and head to it.

When I get to her room, her parents are sitting there with masks on their faces. I'm not going to bother because I spent the night before last inside her, balls deep and my mouth on every inch of her. If I didn't get it then, I won't now. It doesn't even matter at this moment because I need to see if she's okay.

"Carter," she chokes out. Her voice is harsh, probably from the vomiting. I rush to her side instantly without bothering to greet her parents. I'm sitting on the bed, caressing Carly's cheek. My heart's breaking as I look down at her.

"Carter," she moans again. Fuck, I'm sending up prayers that she'll be okay.

"My sweetheart, I'm sorry." I brush a sweaty strand of hair out of her face.

"Don't say I told you so."

"I'm not. You had no clue the kids had it. I just want you to feel better. Damn, sweetheart, I need you to be okay."

"Don't leave me, please."

"Never." I watch her vitals, which are under control. A thought that she's pregnant flashes across my mind, but I know it's too soon to tell. At least not definitively, but we made love more than once without anything between us.

Her parents finally approach me as she falls asleep. "Hello, Carter. I'm so glad to finally meet you," her mother says.

"Sorry, Mrs. Reynolds, I had to check on her. I forgot my manners."

"That's not what I meant. It's wonderful to see how

you care for her. She has mentioned her frustrations once or twice."

"Oh."

"I told her it wasn't what she thought, but one can't see what's in front of them."

"So, when are you going to marry my daughter?" her father asks.

"When she's ready." I'd do it tomorrow, but she's sick and probably needs a little persuading. I'll get her to see my way when I have her in my arms and bed.

"Oh, goodness. She's stubborn. That may never happen," her mother bemoans. I laugh because I agree. She may be a sweetheart, but she's tough as well. Carly is the perfect mix of sweet and strong.

"It will."

"Way to go, son," her father says, patting my shoulder.

"I know she has a brother. Where is he?"

"He was here earlier. He had to leave because Carly wants him to take over the bakery, so he's got a lot to do before tomorrow morning."

"Okay, I'm going to be in the hospital, so I'd like her to stay at least another day or two. Her vitals look good, and from her chart, I can see she's been given meds. If she's improving, they'll let her go, but I'll see what I can do."

"She can come home with us. You can as well."

"Thank you, I'll do what I can. I'm on duty for several days starting tomorrow morning."

"We're going to get something to eat. Are you staying with her?"

"I'll be here all day and night. I already have spare clothes here for my shift."

"You're going to be good for her."

"She's great for me." I love and need her.

They leave, and I bend my head down to her chest, listening to her breathe. It's a little rough, which tears me apart. I long to hold her, but I don't want rumors flying around this place. I cover my sweet Carly with the blanket and kiss her forehead. She needs her rest no matter how much I want to just talk to her. I get up and take a seat in the chair near the window. It's too far away for me. I lift it, then set it next to her bed. I take her hand and hold it in mine as I sit and watch her.

Hours pass with her parents coming in and out. They go home for the night, and I promise to keep them up to date should anything change. Carly wakes up several times, but only long enough for a few smiles.

"Doctor, here you go." Ivy comes in with two orderlies and a rollaway bed. "Thought you could use this."

"Thanks, Ivy. You're not as bad as I thought." I toss her a wink.

She flips me off, then says, "We need you to be on your toes. We already know your mind is going to be focused on her, but at least you can get some sleep."

Chapter Nine

Carly

I push the covers off me. I've been in my old bedroom at my parents' for almost a week, and I hate it. I'm missing Carter every second I'm here. It's frustrating and gut-wrenching. How did I become so needy? He's called several times a day and has come over before or after work and will be here tonight, but I'm feeling so lonely that my heart hurts all the time. This isn't like me and I don't care for this feeling in the least.

My face feels wet and I realize I'm crying, silent tears streaming down my face. We haven't made love all week. My body longs for him, but he's been so good at avoiding my attempts. I feel like driving to his place to see if there's someone else. I don't believe there is, but he refuses to make love to me.

I jump in the shower. Maybe I can wash away the pain and frustration. What's wrong with me? I know I'm in love with him. There's no doubt about that, but there has to be more pulling me out of my mind like this, hasn't there?

"Carly," I hear my mother calling.

"I'm in the shower," I yell.

Her voice gets closer, so I assume she's in my bedroom now. "Your father and I are meeting your brother for dinner before he goes back to Palace. Do you want to go?"

I turn off the spray so I can answer. "No, Mom. I don't feel like it. Besides, Carter said he was going to stop by." I should join Blake for all that he's doing for me, but I'm being whiny and selfish right now.

"Okay. I love you, my angel."

"I love you too, Mom," I reply and then get back to my shower.

A few minutes later, I hear the front door close and then open again. They probably forgot something. Wrapping a towel around my chest and one to cover my hair, I step out of the bathroom. I gasp, shocked to see Carter sitting on my bed.

"Wow, I didn't mean to frighten you. Your mom let me in."

"What are you doing here?"

"I missed you." I rush to him, jumping into his arms and knocking him on his back. He chuckles before grasping my ass. I moan, pressing my hands to his chest then grinding on his length. He grabs my hips and lifts me off him, setting me on the bed. A flicker of sadness crosses my face before I can hide it.

"Don't look sad. I want you more than you can even fathom."

"Then why? Are you afraid of catching something?"

"Sweetheart, I've been around you almost every day. I'm not worried about getting sick, but making you worse."

"Lord, I'm ready to go back to work. I've been cleared," I complain, hoping to persuade him. "Why are you being so...so...? Never mind."

"Yes, you have been cleared, but I don't want to be the reason you relapse. Please calm down before you raise your blood pressure." I'm so mad that I want him to leave. He's being ridiculous. Having to persuade him to touch me feels terrible.

I stand without a word and walk to my large chair near the window and pick up the clothes I'd laid out. "Well, if you'll excuse me, I'll get dressed. Please wait downstairs."

"What? It's not like I haven't seen you naked."

"I'm not saying that. But you don't get to pretend to be attracted to me, then make me feel like I'm begging for it. I'm not going to entertain you with a peep show. If that's not good enough for you, you can leave. I'll join my parents for dinner." I take the towel off my head, letting my hair fall over my shoulders.

"The fuck I'm going anywhere." He rises to his feet, and with three steps he's on me. His mouth comes down on mine while his right hand snakes around my hair and the left lands on my ass, tugging me to his body. "You want me to show how much I need you? Be prepared. I'm going to make you come all night."

He carries me to the bed, pulling the towel off my body, and then climbs above me, his body dominating mine. He grinds his thick bulge against my pussy, driving me wild. I arch up, searching for more, needing his domination because I've missed this so much. Sensing my hunger has grown desperate Carter drops his pants and then slides into me without hesitation.

He bends his head, taking my breast into his mouth, sucking the last bit of water off it. Carter's tongue moves to the other, treating it with the same attention. I buck my hips wildly, my orgasm dancing on the edge. I claw his back, marking him as mine. He looks up, then kisses me with such passion that I don't ever want this to end. A rush of possessiveness blankets me. "Mine," I growl in his ear, causing him to lose it. He thrusts into me repeatedly until I'm coming and he's emptying into me.

There's a huge chance that I could get pregnant, and I welcome it. Fuck me—I'm obsessed with Carter. I can't even understand why I ever hated him. I'm irrationally needy for all things Carter. Having his baby would be perfect.

Chapter Ten

Carter

I call her father to ask for permission. He tells me it's given, and a date is marked on their calendar for next month. The only one I haven't met is her older brother, Blake. Apparently, no one's told him about us because Carly wants to introduce me to him. Even if he doesn't like me, it's not going to stop me. Her parents are already planning our wedding.

I'm back on when I get a call from security. "Dr. James, Ms. Reynolds came in with her parents in tears."

"What?"

"I don't know who they're here to see, but the only major emergency to come through the door was a gunshot victim. He just came out of surgery."

"Thank you, Edgar."

"No problem."

I pull up the lists of patients, and the victim's name is Blake Reynolds. Shit, Carly's brother has been brought in with a GSW. I make my way there as soon as I can. It takes me longer than I'd like, but when I get there, Carly's pacing back and forth, her face flushed. She doesn't look good. The flu is dangerous, and the worst is over for her, but she's getting overly excited and that's putting me on edge. She could be pregnant with my kid. We've fucked like bunnies with no protection. I'd been thinking about it when she was in the hospital. The vision of her round with my kid would be so fucking sexy. I never thought about finding a woman I'd want to have my babies before, but now it's all I can think about with Carly.

"Carly, sweetheart," I whisper, running into the room and wrapping my arms around her. She sobs into my chest. "Calm down. You're going to get sick."

"I'm fine. He's not. I'm worried about him." She's looking up at me, and I want to kiss away her pain.

I wipe her tears, kissing her softly. "I'm more worried about you."

"How many times do I have to tell you I'm all better?"

"You don't fucking look like it. I don't want you pacing. You need to remain calm."

She scrunches her face, pulling out of my arms. Then she lets loose on me. "You idiot. That's my brother. Fix him or I'll..."

I tug her back into my arms, slamming her roughly against my chest. "You'll what, sweetheart? He's going to be fine, but you, on the other hand, should be fucking lying down and resting." She's being irrational, something I completely understand.

"I don't need to lie down," she snaps at me. I roll my eyes because she has no idea that she's pushing my limits. No one means more than she does.

"You're carrying my kid. You'll do as I fucking say," I warn her, grabbing her arm and taking her out of the room. As soon as we get into the hall, I throw her over my shoulder. She fidgets, so I smack her round bottom. She's lucky she's wearing pants because if someone were to see her luscious ass, she'd get spanked. "Quit squirming around."

"Let me down," she screeches.

"Nope." Catcalls and cheers erupt in the hallway as I wait for the elevator.

"Where are you taking me?" she asks, slapping my ass when the door closes.

"To my office where we can talk."

"You can put me down now."

"Are you going to fight me?"

"No." I set her down and intertwine our fingers. The floor's mostly empty, so we make it to my office without being interrupted. I close the door and walk us to my desk, sitting her ass on it, my thighs trapping hers.

"How are you feeling, sweetheart?"

"I'm okay, except that my brother's just been shot by some fucking nutjob."

I place my hands on the sides of her face, holding her still and looking deep into those beautiful blues. "Calm down, my sweet Carly. You're going to make yourself sick. I've checked his record. He'll to be out of here tomorrow."

"He will?"

"Yes, now give me a kiss and tell me you're going to take it easy." She arches her brow, but I'm not fazed one bit. I wrap her legs around my waist and grind my cock against her mound. "Are you going to?"

"Do you think you can control me with your cock?"

"No. I just want you to relax. And this makes you do that pretty fast." Needing to make her come, I slip my hands inside her yoga pants. My fingers make their way to her soaking wet pussy. "Can you come for me, Carly? For the man that loves you so much he can't breathe without you?"

"Yes, yes. I'm coming," she cries. Her head falls onto my shoulder. "I love you, Carter."

My heart just explodes. I'm going to marry this woman.

A knock at the door interrupts our moment. "Give me one second."

Carly hops off the desk and saunters to my bathroom—one of the many perks of having the director's office. I open the door for Ivy. "Dr. James, you're needed in the ER."

"I'm on my way." I hurry into the bathroom. "Baby, I'm being called."

"No problem. You're an amazing doctor." She kisses me, then leaves. I wash and head to work, thinking I'm the luckiest man alive.

Carly

"Carter, I know you're tired, but are you ready to meet my brother?" I ask. He's been working all night. I even fell asleep in his office as I waited for him to finish his shift.

He slips an arm around my waist and pulls me to him. "Do you promise to come home with me?" The warmth of his breath hits my lips, and I need to taste them. I tilt my head and steal a kiss. He growls and deepens it. The look of fatigue is gone from his eyes.

I want him on the desk right now, which isn't good because the place is bustling with staff. "Yes, of course. I want to say good morning, then fall asleep in your arms."

"Fuck, Carly. I could get used to waking up holding you, then eating your pussy for breakfast."

"You know, it is breakfast time," I say before my brain could stop my mouth. He smiles at me with that look.

It's the one I mistook for arrogance. Now I know he's got wicked thoughts in his head. "You're right." He picks me up and throws me over his shoulder, and we leave the hospital. "We'll visit your brother later. I'm tired and hungry."

We hop into his car and of course, he checks my seat-belt. "I can't lose you, Carly."

"You won't. Why are you so paranoid about that? Did you lose a girl you loved?"

"No. You're the only woman I've ever fallen in love with. When I was four, my dad was in an accident, and his wound got infected. It created a blood clot and went straight to his heart. He was twenty-six."

"I'm sorry, Carter," I say, knowing it doesn't stop the hurt. I caress his arm as he drives. "Is that why you became a doctor?"

He takes my hand and raises it to his lips, kissing my palm. "Yes, I wanted to help. When I was in med school, I fell in love with caring for small children. I was torn apart when my father died, but nothing is worse than losing a child. I saw so many parents suffering that loss while I was interning and decided I would throw everything into being a pediatric doctor."

Unable to stop touching him, I run my hands through his hair. It's so thick with a hint of curl. He hasn't shaved since yesterday morning, and that scruff is coming back. I clench my thighs and focus on our conversation. "You're a great doctor. Everyone says so, and it shows since you're the director."

"I'm thinking of making a change very soon," he admits, stealing a glance at me.

"Yeah? What to?" I'm curious what he's considering. As long as it's not gyno, we're cool. I'm not secure enough to let him dig into bitches' cooches. The women I've seen at the hospital would be lining up at the door for an annual. God, I'm instantly jealous. I take a breath and toss the images of me beating a woman to death to the side.

"I want to open a private practice or at least work in a regular doctor's office. Maybe I can catch something before these kids end up in the hospital, you know?" I breathe a sigh of relief. I'm not sure what it would require for him to become a gynecologist, but I'm glad he's not going to change fields. Then again, he could give me a private examination. I'll save that dirty thought for later.

"Yes, I think that sounds wonderful." I'm doing a happy dance in my head.

"So do I. That means I'll have a regular schedule with time to spend with you," he says, throwing a smile my way.

"I'd love that. The drive from Palace to Houston's not too long."

"No, it's not, but I don't want to work in Houston."

"Wait. Where are you planning to move?"

"To Palace, sweetheart."

"You'd move there for me?"

"Damn right, I would. And just so you know, we're getting married, Carly. I know I haven't asked you yet, but this is a warning that it's coming." My heart's jumping out of my chest. I can't believe he just said that.

My man is too damn cocky for his own good. I need to take him down a notch. "Well, Doctor, I'm not sure I want to marry you."

"Well, you best get there. In fact, I think I'll have to hold out until you do," he says, taking his hand off my thigh.

Fucker. Two can play that game. "That's cool. I already got off anyway. You're the one who's going to be surrendering."

"You want to bet?"

"We'll see, Doctor." I'm totally going to cave in hours. I know I can't hold off. The fucker is going to get his just desserts. I brush my hand across my chest, tucking my hand under the edge of the collar. My fingers graze my breasts. He notices, but we've reached his condo. Good, because he forgot I didn't bring any clothes.

"Challenge accepted, sweetheart."

Chapter Twelve

Carter

Who the fuck made up this stupid rule? She's been a walking temptation all day. We quickly took a nap. I knew I'd fucked up when she took off her pants, blouse, and bra. Then she raided my drawer for a shirt. It hung off her large breasts, her hard nipples pressing against the thin fabric.

I climb into bed and fall asleep. The long shifts and practically sleepless nights and days play into my favor. Fatigue hit me hard, but I had to wake up sometime.

"Do you feel better, Carter, love?" she asks, dipping her chest so I can see her breasts from the top of the shirt. I growl, standing with my cock jutting out. The only thing restraining it is the boxers I have on. Her eyes go straight to my dick. Her mouth widens, and I picture her crawling toward me, eager to take me down deep.

"I feel great, Carly." I grab my cock, stroking it through my boxers. I could come this second.

"Hey, that's not fair. No touching yourself."

"Who says? I didn't. You're more than welcome to do it as well. In fact, I'm sure I'd like to see that." I wag my brows, intentionally licking my lips while staring at her pussy. It's barely hidden under my shirt.

"Asshole."

That I am. "Don't give me ideas. I'm going to shower. You can join me."

"I took one while you were sleeping. By the way, I'm not wearing any panties. Oops. Enjoy your shower." She winks. Damn her. She raises her arms in a purposeful stretch. She's not bluffing. Her pussy is on display. I growl and storm into the shower.

I wonder if she can make herself come as fast as I can. She's going to hurt a lot more than me very soon. I take myself in hand, washing and stroking at the same time. I smile to myself, picturing her with her fingers teasing her plump clit, fucking her hand, and pinching her tits.

"Fuck," I roar, coming hard and fast. I rinse and take a towel before walking into the bedroom. I dry my face while my cock hangs free, knowing she's on the bed. Then I get a fucking show when I drop the towel and see her just like my shower image.

Her legs are parted wide on the bed, her heels digging into the mattress. Her long, slender fingers rubbing my favorite treat. I let out a moan, which shakes her out of her mood. I stalk her, climbing onto the bed and between her thighs. I take her fingers and suck them off. She shivers, a pent-up orgasm needing release.

"Say you'll marry me."

"Nope. Was that orgasm good for you? You interrupted mine. I pictured so many delicious things." I'm so stiff again that I've got more than water dripping on the bed. I need her.

"Fuck it," I growl, pushing my way inside her. "I love

and need you, Carly." I pull almost all the way out, then slide back in.

She sucks on my earlobe, then bites it. "I've already picked out my dress, Carter," she whispers.

"Fuck, you are one bad girl," I grunt out, driving deeper into her.

She sighs, moaning with a little giggle. "I love giving you hell."

"As long as I get my heaven. Lips, now," I demand.

"Doctor's orders?"

"Damn right." She gives me the kiss I want, and we're both coming.

Chapter Thirteen

Carly

"Blake, how are you feeling?" I ask my brother as I walk to the hospital bed. Carter is standing at my side, waiting to be introduced, but the look on Blake's face clearly says this will not be friendly.

"I'll be feeling better when I beat his ass."

"Blake," both Amelia and I exclaim simultaneously.

"He knocked up my sister," he hollers, trying to sit up in the bed. Amelia pushes him back, holding his hand to calm him down.

"Technically, I was just hoping," Carter remarks sardonically. He knows my brother's too weak to fight and is not taking him seriously.

The thing is, his hopes were well founded. I had a test done while Carter was working. The lab ran my bloodwork and I'm pregnant, but just barely. It must be from our first night together. "Actually," I mutter.

"Actually, what?" Carter asks.

"Blake, I'd like you to meet my fiancé, Dr. Carter James. He's the pediatric director here."

"Yes, so everyone says. When's the wedding, or are you going to wait until she's nine months?"

"Blake, I love your sister and have for many months now. I get that you're going through a lot, but I'm still going to marry Carly. She's my other half, my better half. Now, I need to have a word with Carly in private."

He takes my hand and walks me out of the room and into an empty lounge area. "Now, do you care to explain the 'actually' to me?"

"Carter, I'm pregnant. Ivy ran the blood test for me." I can barely get the words out before he's spinning me around. I love this man.

"I can't believe it. You're going to make me a dad. Thank you so much, Carly. You're everything to me."

"I love you, too." We kiss over and over, our hands roaming to the point that I have my hand under his dress shirt and he has his hand underneath my skirt.

A cough stops us. I turn to see my father looking at us, holding back vomit or at least pretending to be.

"Did you tell him?" my mom squeals.

"Yes, mother," I sigh, rolling my eyes.

"I can't wait for March seventeenth," he says. It's the day we're getting married. My mother has been getting things together because Carter doesn't want to wait, and now with the baby coming, it seems pointless to anyway. My belly will be too noticeable in a few months.

"Me either. Now let's go tell crabby pants. And I need to call my mother. She'll go bananas."

"Oh, yes. She's got personality and loves you to pieces."

"I know she does. After all, she traveled for scones and a wife for me."

"I'd say she did a good job."

"That is an understatement—fantastic, brilliant, amazing. Any of those will do."

Chapter Fourteen

Carter

I've waited a lifetime for her. Standing at the altar, I feel a million emotions. Number one is excitement. I want to rush into her dressing room and carry her to the priest. Our mothers are walking up the aisle, giggling. They smile at me, then take their seats. I know the time is upon us. The music starts, and my heart is dancing.

She comes out on her father's arm. Her long, blonde hair drapes over one shoulder in a fancy braid. White and pink flowers are intertwined in her hair, making a subtle and elegant crown. The dress. Well, hell, I'm glad I didn't see it before now.

She's spectacular in a floor-length flowy ball gown with a hint of lace around the collar and edge of the sleeves. She shines, and I can't stop staring at her. She's my forever. I'll do everything I can to keep her at my side.

Her father hands her to me with no hesitation. I love that I've been welcomed into the family. Well, not so much by Blake. It took a week or two for him to fully come around. He loves his sister to pieces, and I appreciate it. But as he's there to love and care for Amelia, I'm here to do the same with Carly.

"Keep treating her like she's a princess."

"Always, sir."

The ceremony continues sluggishly for nearly an hour. I want us to have some time alone so I can hold her. She's my world. As soon as the best part comes, I dip my bride and kiss her like she deserves.

"I love you, Mrs. James."

"Say it again."

"I love you," I repeat.

"All of it," she whispers.

"I love you, Mrs. James." She slams her mouth on mine and I scoop her up, carrying her out of the church before we go a bit too far.

"We'll meet you at the reception," I call out. We're going to be late—very late.

Epilogue

Carter

Six months later...

I wash my hands, then come out of the bathroom. "Damn, you need to stop sneaking into my office."

"I can't help it, Doctor. I need you so badly," she moans, coming up to me and tugging on my tie. "Here's a present for giving me what I need," she purrs.

I see the box from her shop. "Thank you, sweetheart." I rub her growing belly. The summer heat has turned my lovely wife into an addict. Since we've been together, I've hated spending so much time away from her. In an effort to have more together, I've joined a local doctor's office as a pediatrician and work once a week at the hospital. It's less money, but we have more than enough to get by.

"I love being your sweetheart," Carly says, brushing her hands up and down my chest. I shiver like it's the first time she's touched me. This woman has my heart and all my desire.

"I love you. You're everything I've ever wanted. How are you feeling?"

"I'm wonderful, but sleepy now."

"Are you headed to the bakery?"

"No, sir. I'm finished for the day. Courtney's closing."

"Good. Are you going home to rest?"

"Yes, and I'll be waiting for you in our room."

"Woman, don't make promises that get me hard all over again. I've got another four hours of patients to see."

"Well, you know I love giving you hell."

"I love your version of it, sweetheart. Get your ass ready for me. Tonight's going to be a rough one."

"I'll be waiting."

God, I'm so glad we bought a house in Palace. It's the largest home around. We got it a week after the wedding because fuck if I could handle traveling all the way to Houston, thinking about her pussy.

Epilogue

Carly

Ten Years Later...

A decade together, and the man hasn't changed one bit. His love for me is even stronger. With every baby, he becomes more growly and territorial. Carter feels like I'm spreading myself thin with three kids and the bakery expanding, but I've hired a few more employees.

I didn't tell him one is a guy. He's getting his degree and wants to intern for me. I couldn't pass up an opportunity like that. I'm planning on telling him when I get home today. At thirty-one, no younger guy is interested in me, but I know my husband will freak.

I'm in my office doing paperwork for the night when I hear, "Who the hell are you?" Shit. I close my eyes, then get up to stop the doc from losing his mind.

"Carter, what're you doing here?" I ask the love of my life as he hulks over my employee.

He looks in my direction, tilting his head. "Carly, there something you want to tell me?"

I stand just off to the side of my intern. "Of course.

Tucker, I'd like you to meet the husband I mentioned earlier."

"Carter, this is the intern from my college," I inform him.

He scrunches his brows before saying, "They sent over a guy."

"Guys do bake, Carter." I roll my eyes because he's being rude.

"So, you're gay?" he asks Tucker.

"Carter," I scold, completely embarrassed.

"No, I'm not. And although your wife is hot, I'm not into married women," Tucker replies with a smile.

"You better keep it that way," Carter growls, nearly lunging at him, but I stop him with a hand on his arm.

"No problem, doc. Now, if you'll excuse me, I need to leave for the day," he says, walking past us to go wash up.

Carter closes the distance between us, crushing his mouth to mine. I pull back and say, "Carter, I'm about to close. Where are the kids?"

"I dropped them off with your parents," he whispers with a smirk.

"Why?" I ask, twisting my lips. I love this man. I wonder what he has in store for me.

"Sweetheart, I want you to myself tonight," he groans, rubbing his cock on my stomach. I want him too. A moan escapes my lips whenever he touches me. I can't help it, and Carter knows. That's why he does these things to me.

"It's nice to have a night alone."

"I'm going to make you come for me. Do you want to do that?" His hand slides between my thighs, effortlessly gliding back and forth.

"Yes," I gasp, trying to hold it together. "Carter, stop. Tucker's still here."

"Well, he needs to get the fuck out because I've got to remind you what happens when you make me jealous," he utters against my ear, sucking on my lobe.

"I'm out, boss," Tucker hollers.

"Let me lock up behind him."

"I'll do it. Lose the panties. When I come back, your ass better be bare for me. Doctor's orders, Mrs. James." I clasp my thighs together. I'm so turned on that my panties are soaked. I reach under my skirt and slide them down my thighs. Thinking of what he's going to do to me sends mini-spasms through my core.

He comes back into the kitchen, and I hear his belt being unbuckled. I lean over the table, resting my elbows on the cold steel with my ass in the air. I feel his hands run up from the back of my thighs. "Mine."

He bends down behind me, running his tongue up my inner thighs. He licks my pussy, and I jump. Carter grabs my ass roughly before spanking one cheek, then the other. I'm gushing with the need to come. The feel of his fingers rubbing my slit before pushing deep inside has my legs shaking. He gives one more swipe of his tongue before standing and thrusting his cock inside me.

"Mine," he growls against my ear, leaning over me and clutching my breasts. He flicks my nipples through my blouse, and I'm done. My body shakes repeatedly as I come on his cock. I feel jets of his cum filling me. He pulls out and pushes my legs closed.

"Keep them like that. I want another baby inside you." I moan as he grabs my panties and works them up my legs. "Don't want my cum falling out." He kisses my ass, then fixes my skirt. "Do you need me to do anything for you?"

"I have to clean up a little. Can you turn off all the lights in the storefront?"

"Already done, sweetheart."

"Great. I'll be back in a few." I get my things and turn off all the appliances and my office light. He leads the way out, and I hit the light by the door.

"I love you, sweetheart. I'm sorry I got jealous."

"Don't. Okay, maybe not with people who aren't doing anything, but I adore the way you love me, Carter. I'd wished I'd seen it sooner."

"Carly, I've always been there and will be forever." He opens the car door. "Now get inside. That's an order."

"Yes, Doctor."

Sweet Surrender

Introduction

This is the third book in the Sweetheart's Treats Series. Although it can be read alone, you may want to read them in order.

Derek: Being a single dad has never been easy, but I've never regretted my decision to keep my daughter and raise her alone. I regret how it happened, but never her. Now that she's grown, maybe I should start looking for the one who will make me happy. Unfortunately, I've found her, but she's too young and too perfect for an old jaded man like me.

Tracy: Why does he do this to me? He's a hardheaded jerk, but I can't let my feelings for the sheriff go. He's always around, but I guess living in a small town it's only natural. I wish that he wouldn't though because my heart can't take this. Leaving town may be my best bet, but I don't think I have it in me to leave. Something has to give. Will they finally admit their feelings, or will they miss their greatest opportunity to be happy?

This is a face-paced fictional novella with possible triggers.

Tracy

I tie my long brown hair up and clean my hands before applying a coat of pink lip gloss to my plump lips. I've just moved here from Houston after running from a life of loneliness. At twenty-three, I'm a waitress at a tiny diner in the heart of a small town called Palace, Texas.

It's a completely different world than Houston. Everything is mostly peaceful and laid back. Recently there has been a string of small burglaries, but no one has been harmed. I love this place and could live here forever. I hear the chime of the front door opening. It's time to begin my day.

Looking over my appearance in the bathroom mirror, I smooth down my pale green dress, then fix my nametag so that it's straight. Tracy. That's my name. My curves are too much for this short dress, but it wasn't like they had much for me to choose from.

The turnover rate isn't high in a small town. Many of these people have been here their whole lives. I took the best fit, but my breasts are a little snug. In fact, it's snug all the way through.

The first thing that comes to mind is what Sheriff Wright would think of my outfit. Where that thought comes from bothers me, but I'm not going to analyze it. I walk out of the bathroom and toss everything into my little locker. They have just enough for the six employees. Standing there, tucking his things into another locker, is an older gentleman. "Hello, I'm Carl, the head cook here. It's a pleasure to meet you."

"I'm Tracy. As you can see," I giggle out when the older man smiles. I feel like a dork because my name is clearly written on my tag. I frankly hate my name, but what can I do? I politely nod to my coworker, then walk around him to get the day started. It's early in the morning, and I've already made an ass of myself. I'm afraid of what the rest of the day will bring.

The place is swamped. I look around to see the two other waitresses are busy at the counter, so I go to the owner and ask what tables mine are. I've got the booths along the wall. Okay. That's almost half the tables in the diner.

"This is going to be fun," I grumble to myself. It's not that I haven't worked as a waitress before, but it's not a job for the lighthearted. Your feet are sore and swollen by the end of the night after doing a hundred trips in an hour. Heaven forbid your customer forgets to request something after you were just there. Then again, small towns are different; they had set ways.

I go about the morning until about ten when two cops walk in. I recognize one immediately. I've seen him every day since I arrived, but we haven't met: Sheriff Derek Wright. The man is fine as hell. He has thick black hair without a hint of gray in it and hazel eyes that seem to change with his clothes. Today he has a little scruff going on. When I saw him with a five o'clock shadow, I thought it was because he didn't have time to trim up, but maybe he's keeping the rugged look. I clench my thighs together. If he did keep it, I'd be a pathetic mess very soon. I have an insane crush on a man that's lived a full life already. He's over a decade older than me and apparently has a daughter a few years younger than me. There's no Mrs. Wright in the picture, but it's not like I'll ever tell him I'm interested.

I walk up to their table, feeling all the hesitation humanly possible seep into my bones. The sheriff gives me a hard look. I don't know what he means by it, but I try to hold myself together. Then the younger one smiles at me, and I relax. I can focus on him for the rest their visit. That way I'll make it through without bumbling my words.

Derek

I walk into the diner, ready for a very hearty breakfast. I don't cook, and my daughter's already on her way to work. Thanksgiving just passed, and I can't eat another damn piece of turkey. I want some steak and eggs. My deputy and right-hand man, Joseph Waters, joins me. We take up our usual booth next to the window.

I see a *For Sale* sign on the building across the street. I hope someone buys it; that way, the town remains strong. If Amelia's interested, maybe she could start a business. I'll have to mention it to her. She's smart and in her first year of college. I've got a great 401K nest egg that would help her if she really wanted to do something like that. It's a random idea, but it might be interesting to look into.

"Thinking about switching your line of work, Chief?" Waters questions.

I look at his smirking face and reply, "No, but I don't want the town to start having that abandoned feel to it. You know there's been a handful of burglaries in the past year, and I take pride in keeping this place wholesome."

"I understand that. I've got high hopes for a great future here. I like this town. I've heard that they're advertising for buyers in Houston for all the vacant properties. You know, where the big money is."

"That would be good." I look around, and the place is a little crowded this morning. Then I catch my breath because the most beautiful woman in the world works here. I have no idea when she started, but I'm pissed that I've missed a chance to see her.

Her long chocolatey colored hair is wrapped up in a high ponytail, taking it away from her heart shaped face, but it doesn't hide any of her beauty. No, it only adds to the fantasies I've had about her.

"Hello, Officers. What can I get for you?" She gives us a killer sweet smile that makes my balls ache.

I swallow hard, but the only thing I want from her isn't on the menu. I've seen her three times in the past three days. She doesn't know that, though. I've been doing all I can to avoid an actual meeting.

I know that I'll end up doing or saying something fucked up to piss her off. My heart's doing shit it's never done before. I have to leave her alone. She's too young for me, and that means completely hands off.

"Good morning, Tracy. It's a pleasure to get my day started with such a beautiful sight." I turn my glare to my deputy. He's about to get suspended for hitting on someone while in uniform. At least, that's the fucking excuse I got. Either that, or I'm going to beat his ass.

"Thank you," she replies, smiling at him. And I lost my appetite. He smiles back at her, and there's not much I can do to fight back the urge to deck him. Taking him out back and dropping him is quickly becoming more appealing by the second.

"Excuse me, but we need to order. I'll have the two-egg and steak platter with a cup of coffee." I know my tone is rude, but what did she expect? She's fucking sexy as hell, and I'm about to lose it because she's intentionally ignoring me. Tracy's giving him the attention she should be giving me.

"Okay, I'll put that order in." She walks away with a little more attitude, but I brush it off. Instead, I'm focusing on her ass that fits so damn perfectly in her green waitress uniform.

"I'll have the same thing, but medium rare," Waters hollers out since she stormed away without taking his order. Tracy freezes, turning around with a blush-stained face.

"Sorry. I'll get right on that, Officer Waters," she murmurs sultry-like. This time she walks away with less attitude but adds a sway to her hip. I'm internally growling because I know that she's going to have men ogling her as she does her job. I finally turn my head to Waters, who's eyeballing me.

"Derek, what gives?" he asks, cocking his brow.

"She's not a piece of meat," I snarl. I can see his mind working it out, but I can't let him know. This town is too small. Everyone would know before I got out of work today. She's too young for me and I should stay away from her, but everything in me demands otherwise.

"Wow, you've never stopped me from complimenting the old waitress here. It's nice to bring a smile to a woman's face. Despite what you think, they like knowing that they're pretty. Maybe you should just ask her out already."

"I am not going to ask out a little girl. She's not pretty, by the way," I add as a side note. I could kick myself when she came from behind me with the coffee pot. Shit. She flips our cups without a word and pours. I want to apologize, but it wouldn't do any good because she wouldn't believe me. Besides, it wasn't as if we could be together anyway.

"Wow, you're racking up the points, boss. You better quit while you're ahead, or you'll end up with coffee dumped on you," he teases, pouring creamer into his cup.

I'm ready to lose it, but what can I do? In all honesty, I want to fuck her on every surface in this place. The thought of splaying her out on the table as my personal meal sounds wonderful. Then hearing her cry out my name as I plow my thick, long cock into her tiny pussy until she comes for me. I'm lost in thought when she stops back at our tables with the hot pot of coffee. She silently refills our cups, refusing to make eye contact with me.

We start talking business until our food comes out a few minutes later. The owner brings out our plates. He usually does, and normally I wouldn't be bothered, but that takes away from seeing her again. "Hey there, fellas. How's it going?"

"It's going great. The sheriff, here, is being a real sunshine this morning." They both chuckle because they know I'm not a morning person. "Wow, these look perfect," Waters says, eyeing his steak and eggs.

"It's on the house, fellas," Mitch says, tapping the back of my seat.

"No, you know we can't do that," I argue.

"Did you not hear what I just said? It's on the house. If you want, you can blow your money giving tips to the waitresses. Enjoy your meals, fellas," he responds, clapping his hand on Waters's back. He walks away with a big grin on his face. She can have all my money. If she wanted, I would give her all I had and ask for nothing in return.

I'm that fucked already. And yet, I have to fight it. She's too young. I should try to date someone my own age. At thirty-six, she probably finds me decrepit. That's why she's flirty with young Waters over here. He's a decade younger than me and without any attachments.

I don't see her again as we eat. Maybe it's her break time, or she's avoiding me and my dickhead comments. We're almost done when she comes out to serve the other waiting customers. When she makes it back to our table, she has that beautiful smile directed at Waters. I grumble to myself, irritated and jealous beyond belief.

"This meal was the best I've ever had. Did you make this?" he asks, smiling like a fool.

"No, but I'll tell Carl you enjoyed it." She freshened up her makeup, I see.

We leave, both of us dropping a twenty on the table. I want to kiss her goodbye like a love-fucking-sick puppy, but I get ahold of myself before I do something stupid.

I make it through the day easily enough. I keep Waters busy and out of my sight so I don't *accidentally* choke him. Mentally, I've done it at least once today.

By the time I get home, Amelia's back from school and cooking dinner. "Hey, pumpkin. How was your day?" I ask, walking into the kitchen.

"It was good." She's a good girl, and I'm forever grateful that her mother left her with me. She's in college, but I know it's not easy to work and go to school. She doesn't have to do both. I've saved enough, but she wants to build character and other than school, there's nothing really to do in this town but work. Most of her friends rushed out of town and never looked back after graduation, but not Amelia.

She feels like she owes me for raising her. It doesn't make sense because it's not as if she doesn't know the truth. There's so much that I need to tell her. I'm not sure if I should even bother to tell her. Enough time has passed where it may be too late.

"Dinner's ready," she says with the sweetest look on her young face. I can't do it. I pass on the opportunity to potentially break her heart.

Chapter One

Derek

Three long months later...

I've been on duty all night after pulling a double. It's time for me to go home, but I can't stop myself from seeing the object of my fascination. I've been in love with her since she first strolled into town. My interest has gotten out of hand. I've essentially become a stalker. As a man of the law, it's not something I should ever admit to and I most definitely should give up this obsession, but I can't.

I'm standing outside the bakery when I get the fucking shock of my life. A woman I missed and yet hoped to never see again is standing there, staring at me with contempt. Of all people, she shouldn't be looking at me like that. Her life is of her own making, and my life is the way it is because of her. She stole my hopes and dreams and made me a man before I was ready.

"What are you doing here?" I ask Emily. I haven't seen her in sixteen years. Amelia's mother gave me custody all those years ago when she abandoned her daughter. I can't fight the anger growing in me. If Amelia sees her, the cat will be out of the bag. And that's not something I'm prepared for. Amelia's coming back to work today and is my excuse for coming here.

She smirks at me, and I hate that I hate her. "I found out my daughter is married to a rich man," she explains, as if that justifies her barging into her life. I have to get rid of her before she gets her hands on sweet Amelia. She wants to use Amelia, and that's it.

"Go away, Emily. She's not your daughter. You gave up that right a long time ago," I remind her. She narrows her eyes at me, but I'm not backing down. "Leave before I arrest you."

"Arrest me for what?" she scoffs, brushing her stringy brunette hair back from her face.

"Being a public nuisance," I warn her. She's not in direct violation, but I know she's capable of making a damn scene.

"Oh, because you're the sheriff, you think that you can charge people with fake crimes," she argues, inching closer to me like she's going to cause some drama.

"It's not a fake crime. I know you're here to start some shit, and by the look of you, you're on some shit."

"I'm not going anywhere until I see my daughter," she howls. And I blanch because one of the few people I don't want to be here is standing behind her.

She catches my gaze, gives me a look, then spins around and locks onto Tracy's face. "Sheriff," Tracy says, walking to the bakery door.

"Good morning, Ms. Hope." Tracy's looking pissed and a bit curious.

Emily leers at Tracy, then back at me. "Oh...I see what's going on. She's your dirty little secret. She's the same age as my daughter."

"I don't know what you're talking about. I have no interest in her."

Tracy's lips twist, and she just rolls her eyes. "I'm not interested in an old man. You can have your ex-husband back."

"Ex-husband? We were never married." A look comes over her perceptive face. This broad is doped up, and yet she's brilliant. Why didn't she do the right thing and just say fucking no? I can't believe that I still want to help her. "Oh, what the hell? They think Amelia's really your daughter. Maybe you should have told the truth, Derek," she finishes with menace in her voice. I know she's about to say something damning.

"You're a bitch, Emily. I'm not going to tell you again. Go away, and stay away from Amelia."

"I don't have to. She's my daughter, and you stole her from me," she exclaims. I'm ready to kill her when I hear an audible gasp behind me. It's my sweet girl. I turn around to see Blake holding Amelia to his chest as she breaks down in tears.

"So you must be the wealthy son-in-law," she coos, essentially ignoring Amelia and stepping practically in between the two. If Blake didn't have Amelia flush against him, she would have.

"Lady, I don't know who you are, but you need to leave us alone because it's clear as fuck you're after one thing." He walks around with Amelia in his arms and into the bakery. "Sheriff, in here now. You—get away from my family shop," he tells her. I follow Tracy in, then lock the door behind me.

"There's a lot to explain. I'm sorry. I never meant—" I stammer, trying to find the right words, thrusting my hands in my hair, then running them down the back of my neck. I hoped that I would never have to have this conversation. I knew I should, but it's hard to tell someone that all they believed is a lie.

"Never meant to what? Lie to me? Kidnap me?" Amelia snaps at me, tears streaming down her face. I can't be mad at her because I deserve her ire. If I could take it back and start over, I would have told her when she was ten.

"I'm going to give you all a moment," Tracy says. I don't want her to go, but I'm not going to beg her to stay. Carly starts walking out of the kitchen, but Tracy pushes her back in, saying, "Family issues." Carly is the owner of Sweetheart's Treats bakery, and Blake is her brother, who just married my daughter. I respect them all, so it's doubly hard to admit how much I've failed my little girl.

"Well?" Blake says to me.

"There's so much to say. But I'm going to tell you what she said wasn't the truth—at least not all of it. I didn't steal you. I had her surrender custody of you when you were a little girl. Around five. It was right before we moved here. I should have told you when you got older, but it's not something I like to talk about."

She uses Blake as her support. He holds her by the tops of her arms. I respect him even more. "So why did you force her to give me up? Why? Did she cheat on you and it was payback or something?" I suppose that's a woman's perspective. Most mothers wouldn't abandon their children unless they were forced to do it.

"No. Please, just listen. That woman out there is not my ex-wife, girlfriend, or anything of the sort. She's...my older sister." Amelia gasps, and so does two voices behind me. It seems that they couldn't stop being nosy. It's okay, because I want Tracy to know me, and explaining this more than once is not something I want to deal with. "Come on, girls. Come over here so you can hear the story better." I wave them over, then rub my hand over my face.

Amelia looks out toward the window, but Emily is gone like she's always been. I know she's on drugs; the shit's written all over her strung-out face. I reach out and grab Amelia's hand, squeezing it in comfort for whatever it's worth. "I'm so sorry about all of this. My parents died at the beginning of my senior year. I turned seventeen and was legally old enough to care for myself. My sister ran out three years before with her boyfriend at eighteen, cutting us out of her life. She wanted nothing to do with rules or obligations at all. My parents cut her out of their will and as a consequence, I received everything, including the house. About a month before my graduation, she showed up with you and the police. She'd been living on the streets of Houston hooked on drugs. The guy who she left with had got her doped up. He's supposedly your birth father, but he had never been on the birth certificate and therefore the reason she came to me. If I didn't take you both in, they would arrest her and take you into state custody. I had a choice to make. It wasn't easy because I had plans for college, but from the first moment you smiled at me, I knew that I couldn't let you suffer like that. You had suffered enough. I never regretted having you in my life."

She lets go of Blake and rushes into my arms. I wrap her up and hold her tight. "I can't tell you how sorry I am that I didn't tell you sooner. I worried that your father would come looking for you, so I lied to people about it. After leaving my sister pregnant and drugged up, I knew he didn't deserve to take you from me. I finally got her to give you up for the last of my parent's inheritance. I may be your uncle, but to me, you've always been my daughter."

"I'm sorry, Daddy," she mutters, pressing her head to my chest. I love her so much.

"You've nothing to be sorry about. I've loved you from the first time I held your little body in my arms." Blake pulls her back to him with his hand around her waist. He loves her, and I know he'd die for her. We saw it happen just a few weeks ago when her stalker came after both of them. I'm forever indebted to him for saving my little girl. He reaches out a hand to me, and I shake it.

"Thank you, Mr. Wright. Without you doing what you did, I wouldn't have met the love of my life," he acknowledges. That's one of the many blessings I got for making that hard life choice.

"But you never got to live your own life. Have your own son or daughter. I can't believe that you never tried to find anyone," she says, feeling guilty. I smile at her because yes, I didn't have my own child or watch my wife carry our baby, but I'm not that old.

"I know you think I'm ancient, Amelia, but I'm only thirty-five. I've got plans to get married and have a bunch of kids."

"How? I've never seen you date."

"You're right. I haven't since you came to live with me. At first, I was just trying to hang on and do everything right by you. When you were about ten, I wanted to start dating, but as a cop, my life wasn't easy to maneuver around. Then, I didn't know how."

"Well, I'm married, and you can go and get anyone you want." She insinuates that there's already someone. I wonder if she knows. I look around to see that although Carly's still standing around, Tracy's nowhere to be found. "I'm sorry, Dad. I know you're tired. You should be going home to rest. How about we stop over after work?" she offers.

"I'd like that. I need to go before I pass out driving." Reminding me that I should be exhausted did the trick. I lost the second wind I had a moment ago. I walk out without saying goodbye to my woman. I'll check on her in a few hours. I need some sleep, though. As soon as I get home, I fall asleep on the sofa.

Chapter Two

Tracy

I watch in awe at the scene in front of me. I can't even deny the initial jealousy that stole my breath when she referred to Amelia as her daughter. The rumors and stories had been that she'd left him to raise a kid. I suppose that she had, but the relationship status was incorrect. Amelia became his because he was the only family she had left. Damn, that makes him one hell of a man. I can't imagine someone giving up their happiness at such a young age.

A wide variety of emotions pour right through me. I can't say that I even know how to handle them. The wisest thing for me to do is go about my work. I slip back into the kitchen during the exchange between Blake and the sheriff.

There's a lot of work to do for the day. I'd quit working at the diner last week after the shooting since they needed my help at the bakery. Baking is the only thing that occupies my thoughts away from the sheriff. I've been in love with him from the first day we met. I put my headphones in and put on my favorite playlist and try to drown out my thoughts.

It's been a long day, but all my pastries came out perfect, surprisingly so. My mind has been focused solely on Derek and the revelations that he shared. Amelia's a mix of happiness and sadness all in one today. She wavered through the emotions as she randomly mentioned things throughout the day. This isn't the Amelia I met before. She was confident and happy, but I can understand her confusion. Like her mom, my parents were on drugs and I was taken away from them. I lived with my Grandma until two years ago when she died. It was soul crushing and left me wanting to be alone. Even though we didn't have a large apartment and lived modestly, she kept a huge secret from me. Last month, I found out that in two years, I'll be wealthy. Well, at least very well off. She had a trust made for me that would be available when I turned twenty-five. The lawyers couldn't find me until now because I've been moving around, trying to find somewhere that could take away the pain of losing her.

And for the first time in forever, I feel like I'm home. Maybe that's because the sheriff is always lurking, looking after me, making me smile even when I'm frustrated with him. He refuses to call me by my name and always keeps it formal. Except for that one time...he told me I couldn't work at the bakery because he said so. I laughed him off because he's not my keeper. I still haven't figured out what his problem was, but I think it had to do with Blake in general and his daughter. He was worried about her and didn't trust Blake.

Chapter Three

Derek

It's been a long week since I ran into Emily. She hasn't contacted Amelia again, so I hope she ditched her attempt to get money from her. I've been doing my best during my patrols to check on Tracy and Amelia. I didn't want Emily to try to hurt them for money. Truthfully, I'd make an excuse to see Tracy. Although most of the time, she doesn't see me.

Like the stalker I am, I follow her home just a minute behind her. Every day I want to knock on her door and pull her into my arms, kissing her like she needs. She's got her keys in her hands, holding them like a weapon with a key between her knuckles. Smart girl. I watch her slip the key into the lock and turn it. I don't always get to do this because I'm at work, but I need to know if she's safe.

Her door slams awkwardly, and through the window I see shadows. I hear her scream, and that's when I see what's going on. Two guys are shuffling around her apartment. Immediately, I call for backup. "I need backup 22 N. Central. Two guys—looks like a B & E."

"On the way." Gun out, I rush up the stairs and slam straight into her apartment. I fire off a shot at the one holding my woman, hitting him in the arm. He lets go, then both of the assholes take off running before I can fire the next shots in their heads. They dash out the rear exit of the apartment and down a flight of stairs. "I'm in pursuit," I say into my walkie, running after them.

I see them hop into a waiting car. I try to position myself before firing since there are children in this area, but they speed off with a third person in the driver's seat. Instantly, I radio my men to give them all the details I can. Since it's dark out, I can't make the exact color of the vehicle, but I know it's a Chevy Tahoe about ten years old. I call out the BOLO on it. Then I step back inside. Tracy is shaking and rocking herself in the corner of the living room. I lock the front and back doors, holstering my weapon. I know it's more than a robbery gone wrong.

Walking up to her, I grab her hand and lift her to her feet, then I wrap her up in my arms where she belongs. "I'm so sorry, baby. I'm not going to let them hurt you, *ever*," I promise her with a burning need to protect my woman.

"Derek," she sobs, pressing her head against my chest. With every tear she sheds, my heart breaks. I'm going to hunt these fuckers down myself. The thing is, they were lying in wait for her. I didn't see anything, and neither did she when we both first pulled up. Burglars would have been moving around and bolted like they did when I arrived. I made a mental note that they don't fit the description of the burglars in the area. Something's going on, and I'm going to get to the bottom of it. I rub her back; my heart is racing out of control. This is the moment I've been waiting for forever, just to hold her. Unfortunately, it took me this long to welcome it, and I almost lost her. I let her hold on tighter, releasing a sigh. And I hear my walkie go off.

"Sheriff, we are outside." I forgot that our silhouettes can be seen from where we're standing. That's how I could tell someone had broken in, so my could totally make us out. Honestly, I no longer cared.

"Sweetheart, I need to get you out of here." There's a lot of work to do, but she doesn't need to be here for it. I can question her later about the guys in her place and if she happened to know them at all.

"I don't have anywhere to go," she mutters, looking up at me with those round eyes that captivate me every time.

"Tonight, you're staying with me," I tell her. She doesn't fight me, thankfully. "Sweetheart, you want to go get some things that you'll need?"

"Okay." She reluctantly leaves my arms. Then as equally reluctant, I open the door and let the other officers in.

"Start looking at the scene. There were two guys waiting for her and a third in a car outside. We need to see if there are surveillance cameras around this area."

"I highly doubt it, sir. There's no need for cameras around here. The burglaries are isolated to the other side of town."

"I want you to double-check anyway," I bite out. "I need to go check on Ms. Hope."

I walk back to her room and accidentally catch her changing.

"Shit." I step out and close the door. I'm horny and pissed at the same time. She left her bedroom door unlocked. Any of my men could have walked in there. Right now is not the time to curse her ass out. I'll have to fix that for later, though. I stand guard at the door because fuck if I catch one of my men looking at her. She comes out a moment later with a double bag packed.

"I noticed your apartment doesn't have much in it. You've lived here for a few months?" I ask.

"Yeah not a clutter kind of person," she admits. It's more than that; the place looks empty. There's no reason for the robbers to come here—unless they weren't here for a robbery.

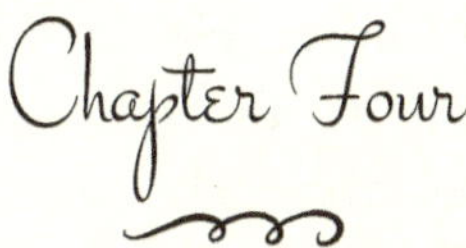

Chapter Four

Tracy

He buckles me up in the passenger seat as if I was a kid and then goes around and gets in the car himself. A myriad of thoughts race through my head. Oddly, the first being—why was he outside my house? It makes no sense since he lives on the other side of town. I wonder if it was by accident, or is there a real reason he was passing by? I'm too afraid to ask because maybe he's going to see the lady that lives next door to me. She's closer to his age than I am, and she's beautiful. They would make a cute couple, which destroys me.

"You know I'm not going to let them harm you, right?" he reassures me. I guess my feelings are on display. He thinks I'm upset about the guys in there. My thoughts at the moment are solely about him right now. I can't tell him that, but they are all about the sheriff.

"I know you won't let them," I answer softly. He turns back and starts driving toward his house. I know he lives close to the edge of town—completely in the opposite direction from my apartment.

"Are you hungry?" he asks.

"No, I'm not, but thank you for asking. And thank you for earlier. I don't know what would have happened if you didn't show up." The fear of what could have happened seeps inside me, and I shiver. He reaches over and grabs my hand as I start to relive the moments before he came bursting through my door. His thumb rubs against the back of my hand, and it feels so wonderful and soothing.

I stay quiet for the rest of the ride because I'm on the edge of an emotional breakdown and don't want him to see it. As if he understands, Derek doesn't ask any more questions. He has a very nice home, I notice as we pull into his driveway. "Well, we're here," he says, releasing a hard breath. Derek throws it in park, then jumps out of the car. He grabs my bag from the back when he comes around for me. His strong, manly body moves effortlessly, and it makes me feel safe to have his hands on me.

He leads me up the stairs and into the house. "Wow, you have a lovely home," I remark. He turns around and smiles at me. "Thank you."

I feel like he wants to say more, but he doesn't. Instead, he heads to the kitchen, but not before asking if I'd like something to drink. "No, thank you." I pause, then change my mind. "You know what? As a matter of fact, I'll have some water."

He smiles at me. "Sure thing." Then he leaves me alone.

I walk around the living room just examining the house. It's full of photos of Amelia and Derek throughout the years. Knowing the truth of his life makes me fall even deeper in love with him. He took on the responsibility that wasn't his own. He's a great man. "Here's your water, sweetheart." I love hearing the endearment.

"What happened to the *Ms. Hope*?" I blurt out. He

blushes and stammers for a moment before saying sorry. “I'm not bothered by it at all,” I tell him. “I'm just starting to think you don't like my name.”

“Tracy,” he says, moving closer to me. I can feel his breath inches from my face. “When I see your name, I think about all the things I want to do to you. I constantly think about you.”

“You weren't over there to see April?” I ask. Externally, I show no emotion. Internally, I’m doing a happy dance.

“No, I wasn't. This is going to sound pretty fucked up, and you're probably going to want to run away. But, Tracy, I'm obsessed with you. I wanted to make sure you got home okay. I often do. I know it's kind of crazy, especially because you're so much younger than I am.”

“Stop. Stop right there. You've been watching me? Staying at a distance all this time?”

“Yes,” he relents. I put my glass of water down on the table. Then I punch him in the arm.

“So for the past three months, you've been making me think that I'm a fool for having feelings for you,” I complain.

He doesn't respond with words. Instead, he pulls me into his arms, lifts me onto his lap so that I'm straddling him, and then pulls my hair and kisses me hard—the kiss that I've been waiting for since we first met. I moan and rock my hips slowly, aching for him. I need Derek more than I can express.

Our lips meld together perfectly. His hands slide down my back, cupping my bottom and squeezing, thrusting me up against him. He pulls back, breaking our kiss for just a moment to say, “You're never leaving me. I've waited too long for you.” He brings my face back to him, kissing me deeper than the first time; his tongue caresses mine until I toss my head back, needing air. My chest presses against his, my firm nipples showing how turned on I am.

He tugs at my top, pulling it off me. He drops his head and sucks on my breast, lowering the cup of my bra down. His teeth drag along my nipple, giving me a sense of what's to come. Derek's tongue circles around my nipple before he sucks it in intensely. It sends delight straight down to my feminine parts. I feel like I'm going to come instantly. I start moving faster on him until I'm screaming his name over and over again, coming harder, deeper than I thought possible. So many lonely nights I've touched myself thinking of him and what it would feel like. It's nothing like what I dreamed of; it's ten times better. "That's it, baby. Fucking hell, yes. Come for me."

Chapter Five

Derek

Watching her come is the best thing I've ever seen. I lose my mind, standing up with her in my arms. "You're not done yet, Tracy. I want you coming around my cock," I growl as I carry her off to my bedroom.

"Yes, please," she pants, moaning and smiling as she kisses me all the way there. I lay her on the bed and then walk over to the chair by my closet to lose my clothes.

"Strip for me," I tell her. I take off my belt, gun, and holster, setting them aside properly. My shoes I kick under the chair and I tug off my socks; the rest of my clothes come off quickly. I'm standing there in all my pride and glory, eyeing her as she undresses. I stroke my cock, squeezing it a little rougher than comfortable to calm myself down. I'm aching to be inside her, fucking her womb. The thought of her having my baby has been in my head since the day we met; I could come from just the idea of her wanting the same. "You're so beautiful, baby," I profess, walking toward the bed.

She blushes, and I need to know this answer before we

go any further. “Are you sure? Because there’s no turning back. Once I’m inside you, that’s it.” She nods her head and wags her finger, beckoning me to come forward. I climb onto the bed, my legs straddling hers with my cock resting on her flat tummy. In all my life, I’ve never been so fucking excited. It's been over sixteen long years since I've had sex, and frankly I can't remember it. I hope I can meet her standards. I can't stop thinking about how much I want to be inside her, and my cock starts leaking small beads of cum on her belly. She bites her lip and looks up at me so wantonly that I can’t believe the next words out of her mouth. “Derek, I’m a virgin.”

I swallow hard, holding back the need to come on her right now. I lean forward, pressing my knuckles into the mattress. I kiss her mouth hard, letting her know how fucking pleased I am with the news. “Scoot up, baby.” She moves up, almost sitting completely against the headboard. Then I grab her thighs and spread them wide. I look down at the present I was given, thinking to myself that I must have been a good boy to deserve this. I run my hands along her soft thighs. She shivers as I do so, knowing what's coming next. I lay on the bed, leaving trails of my own come on the sheets. Laying in between her sweetness, I press my face down to her thatch of curls, smelling her, taking her in, and knowing she's all mine. My need boils inside of me, but I want her to enjoy this as much as I'm about to. Rubbing against the softness of her wet pussy, she moans out gentle pleas for more. “You’ll get all that and more, baby.” My tongue lashes out hitting her right on her clit, making her cry out and pull her knees up in the air with her feet digging into the bed.

She screams and grasps the bedding, bunching it up in her hands as I make her come. It’s the sexiest thing I’ve ever seen. Needing to make her mine, I wait until she's calmed down. I stroke my cock up and down her still pulsating clit, then push the head in a little. The urge to come is almost automatic. I can feel a little come leak out inside of her. I lower my upper body, pressing my hands into the mattress. I kiss her, working her back into a soft moan, then as I deepen the kiss, I take her all the way. She doesn't shed a tear as I take her innocence.

My pride is too full to fuck this up. I want her to come again, this time taking my seed with her. She throws her legs around my waist, her tiny feet digging into the top of my ass. I growl and drive long and slow thrusts into her. She cries out, then pulls my head to hers. We kiss until I feel her womb squeeze my length. I'm so close, but I demand she come with me. "Come again, Tracy. Show me that beautiful look as you come."

She clenches her sweetness again, coming for me and sending me into a hard and fast orgasm. Jets of cum shoot into her womb. I know it's unprotected. The thought of putting my baby in there keeps me stiff.

"So perfect," I whisper to her, kissing her soft lips as we both pant for air.

"You're going to get me pregnant if we're not careful."

"Even better. I want you to give me as many babies as you can."

Chapter Six

Derek

I wake up to the aroma of breakfast being made. My stomach growls; it smells so damn good. Even though I'm exhausted, I climb out of bed.

I'm surprised Tracy found anything to make in this house. I really don't keep a lot of food, especially since Amelia moved out. I stand and stretch, then notice Tracy's still in bed with me. Who the fuck is in my kitchen? I slip on some clothes, grab my gun, and head out.

"Whoa!" Blake shouts. "Put the gun away."

Shit. I set my gun down on the side table. I totally forgot that Amelia still had a key since she comes to check on me to make sure I'm okay. "Hey, Daddy. Just thought it'd be great to make you some breakfast. Do you think Tracy likes sausage or bacon?" My eyes widen because she knows that she's here. "How do you know she's here?"

"Daddy, Carly told me what happened last night when we got to work this morning. And that she was staying with you until the coast was clear." Holy hell, she thinks Tracy's just staying here in a protective custody type of way. She is, in a sense, but it's more than that. I hear footsteps behind me, and I holler before she can even get over here for anyone, Blake in particular, to see.

"Tracy, please tell me you have some fucking clothes on." I hear the footsteps turn around and dash back into my bedroom.

"Whoa. Seems we got more of a celebration going on here, Amelia. We should leave. Love, we've interrupted your dad."

"I'm so sorry, Daddy. I just thought you guys could use someone to look after you after what happened last night. I didn't know that you finally admitted your feelings for her."

"You knew?"

"I think the only one who didn't know it was her. You get all moody and a little bit bossy around her. Besides, I've seen the way you look at her. I've been waiting several months for you to finally ask her out."

"Well, pumpkin. It's more than dating. Tracy's going to be my wife. I hope that's okay with you."

"Okay with me? Daddy, you're old enough to make those decisions yourself. You know you don't need my permission. But I think you should ask her first, you know."

"Yes, it would be nice," Tracy agrees behind me.

I spin around and slip my hands through her hair, fisting her dark colored ponytail around my hand, smiling into her gorgeous eyes. "No, woman. I told you last night it was a done deal—signed, sealed, and delivered, baby."

"Yep, there goes the bossiness again. We'll just leave you guys to enjoy your breakfast," Amelia says. As much as I love having them here, I want to be alone with Tracy because my thoughts are anything but fatherly right at this moment.

"No, no. Don't go. Stay for breakfast with us," Tracy

offers. She's right. We shouldn't try to kick them out, even if that's what I selfishly want right now.

"You and Tracy could discuss the girly things she's going to need," I add.

"I only need you," she whispers in my ear.

Blake grabs Amelia around the waist, then whispers loudly, "Baby, I think it's time we leave; if you know what I mean." He wags his brows and looks toward us.

"Gross. But yeah, let's go. I love you, Daddy. Tracy, girl, I'll talk to you later. Oh, and here. Don't want to be walking in on anything next time." She drops her key down on the counter.

"I love you, pumpkin."

"I suppose it's time for me to finish breakfast really quick," she says, walking off into the kitchen. I'm watching her round ass sticking out of a pair of tiny bike shorts that barely cover anything. When I said to put clothes on, I meant something I wouldn't have to kill Blake for seeing her in. I follow her into the kitchen. Making sure all the burners are off, I grab her around the waist and pull her up against me, wanting her to feel every inch of my ridge as I grind my hips forward. "Do you call these clothes, baby? I can feel how wet you are right now."

"Says the guy wearing only boxers and a T-shirt."

"Don't give me no attitude, woman. I don't want you showing off anything that belongs to me," I murmur, nipping at her ear and sucking it between my lips. "No need to cook right now, baby. I've got all I want to eat right here."

She moans, planting her hands on the sides of the kitchen sink. I lift up her tee just to caress her waist, and she shivers from the tenderness of my hands. Grabbing the hem of her shorts, I slide them down and press my face against the edge of her slit, then thrust my tongue into her folds. She moans, pushing her butt out, opening her legs wider.

I run my hand along her pussy, then spin her around. I lift her legs over my shoulders and continue to eat her sweet core. Her juices coat my tongue, and I suck harder. She grips the counter tight, then clenches her legs around my head, coming and screaming my name. I drink her up until she's coming down from her high.

"Wow, talk about breakfast. I could get used to a meal like that, woman." I stand up and pull my cock from my boxers. Lifting her legs around my waist, I push straight into her depths. We both grunt and I slam my mouth to hers, swirling our tongues together as I pump into her womb. I'm already on the edge, and it won't be long. I need her to come again for me. I lean down, pull her top up, and suck on her hard nipples.

She moans and clenches around me as I switch from side to side. Her body is sweet perfection. A growl roars through me as I hear the telltale orgasmic bliss come from her lips. "I'm coming," she cries out, her hands thrusting into my hair and pulling my mouth to hers. My release is pulled from me as she squeezes my cock over and over again. I lean forward and rest my head on her shoulder.

"Damn, that was fucking incredible," I mutter against her flesh, creating a lovely layer of goosebumps.

"Tell me about it," she sighs, looking very tired. I need to let her lie down a bit longer. Without pulling out, I carry her over to our bedroom, then lay her on the bed.

"Rest a little while. I'm going to jump in the shower."

"Okay," she murmurs, curling up under the messy covers.

I take a long, hot shower because my body feels the last

twelve delicious hours. When I get out, she groggily gets up and goes into the bathroom. "My turn."

While I'm getting dressed, I call the station. "Do you have anything on the car last night?" I ask Waters, slipping on my socks.

"I just got off the phone with Houston PD. They found the car abandoned in a bad part of town. Chief, I'm thinking we're looking at some trafficking ring."

"Are you serious?"

"Prostitutes are huge in that area. And from the looks of her apartment, they weren't there to rob her."

"I'll be in later today to go over more of the details and see if we can't find the person who's involved. They would have to be someone from around here. There's no reason to come here and target her specifically."

"That's very true. Houston PD is under the same impression. They plan to send a couple detectives down to see if we can work this out together."

"Sounds good. What time will they be there?"

"They said about four."

"Okay, I'll be there just before then." I hang up just as Tracy comes out of the bathroom in a towel that barely restrains her large breasts. My dick jumps in my pants, but I know that it's not a smart move. "I've got to make a couple more work calls this morning, then I'm all yours again." I wag my brows at her.

"I'm going to finish breakfast because even though you've had a meal, I'm still hungry," she jokes, winking and sauntering back toward the kitchen.

Chapter Seven

Tracy

I feel bad that I wasn't at the bakery today, but I left a message for Carly last night to let her know what had happened.

Carly called me at six a.m. to see how I was doing. I told her where I was staying. Playfully she made jokes, but promised not to tell Amelia. It didn't matter because she already knows and is cool with it. That was a big worry for me. Amelia and I close in age, but not that close. Everybody seems to think I'm only twenty years old, but I'm already twenty-three. I'm sure that she wants the best for her dad, and I'm happy that she likes me enough to approve.

Breakfast was already halfway done, so I finish it and wait while he makes some work calls. After serving the sheriff dozens of times at the diner, I know what he likes. Just as he comes into the kitchen, I hand him a plate. "Damn, this looks and smells fabulous."

"You're welcome. Amelia did half the work. Enjoy." We both sit down and eat, talking about nothing really.

"I want to ask you something. How come at twenty-three you were a virgin?"

"Bad dating experiences, and then I left my hometown about four years ago. Since then, I've been trying to make things work for me, leaving dating to the side. Besides, for the past year, I've been only interested in a man who did his best to irritate me."

"Sorry about that. Trust me, it's been hard for me too. We need to get a moving truck to your place and have you moved in here as soon as possible," he tells me.

"Aren't you rushing this?" I ask, sipping from my coffee cup.

"Didn't you just say that we wasted months?" He's right about that. I know that I only want him. I may be young, but I'm not naïve.

"We just don't know each other," I explain.

He grabs my hand, intertwining our fingers. It feels so perfect that I don't know if I can walk away. My heart and body belong to him, but I have to be strong. It's a fight I'm not sure I can win. Then he looks me deep in the eyes and begins, "I know that you don't like coffee creamer, you work hard as hell, and that you're way too good for me. And most importantly, I know that I can't live without you."

Yep, I surrender. I nod, smiling. "Then it's settled. I'll move in with you."

He tilts his head, quirking his brows. "Move in? You're more than moving in, Tracy. You're marrying me as soon as possible. Do you have any family and friends that you need to give notice to?"

"No, I don't," I confess.

"Why not?" He brushes my face with the back of his fingers.

"I was raised by my Grandma, but she died two years ago." My eyes water up because I miss her so much. If it wasn't for her, I wouldn't be the caring woman I am today. I would probably be dead or on drugs. That's a scary thought.

"I'm sorry, Tracy. I didn't mean to upset you."

"No, I'm okay. I promise. I'm just happy that I have you now."

"Good, then it can be a small wedding," he adds. I can see his mind moving a million miles an hour and that strong jaw upturning to a show his sexy smile.

I'm completely his. "I suppose, boss man. And when are we supposed to have this wedding?"

"I'd marry you today if I could get away with it."

"Well, then, we better get this together. I want to be your wife, Derek," I answer. I'm so in love with him that it doesn't matter. He grabs my hand and pulls me off my chair and into his lap. He attacks my neck with his lips.

"Marry me this weekend," he says, nibbling on me.

"Yes," I answer, and that's when I feel something metal slide across my finger. I look down to see a very large and beautiful three-stone diamond ring.

"I've had this since we met. I didn't get it in town because some people are too nosy. You know that people gossip around here."

"Yes, I totally get that. I might have run away from this place if I found out, thinking it was for someone else. Having worked in the diner, I can hear what the people say when they are socializing."

"Then I'm thrilled as fuck that I didn't buy it anywhere near here. Speaking of the diner—I know you're not going back to work there, but what about the bakery?"

"It's good, but it's not what I want to do with my life."

"What do you want to do?"

"I'm not sure. When I was younger I wanted to work in law enforcement."

"Really? That's pretty cool. Did you want to be an officer or something else?"

"I wanted to work in Narcotics. After being taken away from my mom because of drugs, I wanted to get the drug dealers off the streets. It's now an insurmountable task, but it's out of the cards. I don't want to spend that much time away from you," I admit. It's scary how much I need him. I've managed to keep myself together, but then he acknowledged his feelings and that was it.

"Good, because I selfishly don't want you in danger. Speaking of, I want you to come down to the station with me. There's a lot of shit that needs to be taken care of before I can let you out of my sight. I won't let anything happen to you."

"There's something I need to tell you as well."

"What, Tracy? You can tell me anything."

"My grandmother had a trust created for me. I get it in two years."

"Really? Well, that will come in handy."

"You're not curious about it?"

"It's not my business. If you want to tell me, then you can, but I'm not going to press you about your money."

"Well, it won't matter because we'll be married."

"You can tell me when you get it, okay?"

"Okay," I agree, kissing him on the lips then hopping off his lap. I still have to clean up the dishes. He's going to freak out that we'll be rich pretty soon. It's not enough to live off forever, but it'll set us up nicely for our retirement and our kids' colleges.

Chapter Eight

Derek

We enter the station, and three of my deputies are present. They all take notice of Tracy at my side. I fucking hate the way they look at her. It makes me want to shoot all of them on the spot. "Let's go into my office." I press my hand to the small of her back and lead her into my office, closing the door behind me.

"What's wrong? Are you embarrassed that they think we're together?"

I laugh out loud. "I put a fucking neon sign that we're together on your finger. Pretty soon, I'm hoping there'll be a very telltale sign that you're mine." I rub my hand on her flat abs. "I'm not embarrassed at all. I want them to stop staring at you. Every damn day since we met, I've been doing all I can not to blind the guys around here," I finish with a grunt. I've never had a reason to be jealous before. Now, it's like even the slightest smile thrown her way is liable to make me lose it.

She expresses her amusement with my territorial behavior. "Makes sense now why you didn't want me to work with Blake. I thought you were just looking out for Amelia."

"Yes and no. I don't want anyone eyeing you like their next meal. You're only mine." She shakes her head and rolls her eyes before taking a seat.

I just take my seat around the desk when I hear a loud commotion in the hall. It's a woman hollering and furniture being kicked about.

I open the door to find my sister being escorted into one of the holding cells, and another guy I clearly recognize being taken into another. I turn to Tracy. "Stay here." I step out and close the door behind me. I don't know what's going on, but I don't want Tracy to get hurt in any way.

"What the hell is going on?" I call out. Deputy Sanchez, the one who just locked up the man, turns to me and says, "These two were caught back at the scene of the crime. We let them sneak in. It seems they were trying to find something they dropped. We have it right here," he chuckles out, holding a small piece of paper with a phone number. It's probably their contact, especially if they were willing to come back for it.

I look over to my sister, who at this moment is so damn high she doesn't even recognize me. "What the hell are you looking at, lawman? I bet you'd like me to service you after hours, right?"

Holy fuck, I don't know whether to be fucking revolted or depressed. I'm feeling both at the moment. "Call me when the detectives arrive," I tell Sanchez. I refuse to look in her direction. Instead, I go straight into my office. I can't believe that woman out there is my big sister. It's a damn travesty what drugs do to you. As fucked as it was that she went after Tracy, something tells me she would be willing to go after Amelia if Blake wasn't around. I wonder if they had staked out the bakery and my run-in with her last week had fucked up her plans. There are so many questions I want to ask, but I can't until she's somewhat sober.

As soon as I'm in my office, Tracy looks up from reading the Houston newspaper that's on my desk. "What's wrong?" I guess I didn't mask the pain in my heart. Fuck. How do I tell her my sister's been arrested on charges related to her attack? Or how she accused me of planning to accost her later? A shiver runs through me in disgust. "Seriously, what's wrong, Derek?" she asks, standing up and walking to me.

My intercom in my office buzzes. "The detectives are here."

"Give me one minute," I respond.

I pull Tracy into my arms for a brief hug, letting her go before she pushes me away. I know that would gut me to feel and witness. "I know this is going to sound very fucked up, but if you want to leave me, I'll do my best to convince you not to go."

"You're scaring me, Derek."

"I don't mean to. The thing is...the woman screaming has been arrested for breaking into your apartment."

"Oh, goodness. Tell me it isn't your sister."

I run my hands over my face because fuck if there's anything I can to do to erase all of this. "She is." Tracy sits down, then starts to get up, then sits back down.

She looks up at me, and concern crosses her face. She stands up and wraps her arms around me. "I'm sorry." My heart drops. She's going to leave me. I can't do this. I can't let her go. Before I can respond, she sees the panic on my face. "I'm sorry about your sister. I'm not going anywhere, Derek. This isn't your fault. I know you love her, but this time you're not paying for her sins. You deserve to be with me if that's what you want."

"It's all I've wanted from the moment I met you. I love you so much, Tracy."

I open the door and let the detectives in. "Hello, I'm Sheriff Derek Wright."

"I'm Dennis Johnson, and this is my partner, Aaron Reeves."

"Let me introduce you to my fiancée, Ms. Tracy Hope," I say, grabbing her hand and pulling her close.

"Wow, this is an interesting development. Have you updated Ms. Hope about the arrest?"

"That's what I was doing when you arrived. Please, let's have a seat." I give Tracy my chair while I stand behind her. The detectives take the seats in front of my desk.

"Well, so here's the deal. We believe they are working for a trafficking ring that abducts women and teens for prostitution. As we speak, the FBI is infiltrating the main operation. They were already onto the group and were about to strike when we contacted them."

"I wouldn't let them traffic me."

"I'm sorry, Ms. Hope, but most of those women who fight, die. Very few escape. It's not like they treat you well. They beat you until you can't fight them, then inject you with heroin until you become compliant and addicted. Then you'll do whatever they say."

"Are you telling me that's what's wrong with my sister?"

"Yes and no. She's been arrested for straight prostitution on the street. She hasn't been trafficked; she chose that life. Although, she may not always have chosen it. She had a chance for help about ten years ago but refused to roll on her handler."

"They refer to that behavior as Stockholm Syndrome. I'm sorry, but it's a strange phenomenon that alters their perception of their captor. Along with the drugs, she may be unreachable."

"Do you think she can get help?" Tracy asks.

"I don't know. She needs a lot of help that she can't get around you all."

"After her time served, if you want, Tracy, we can check to see if she wants to get to know us."

"I wish you all the best. We're going to take them into our custody, if you could please sign them over."

"Of course." I turn to Tracy. "Please stay in here. She's not in her right mind, and I'm afraid of what she'll say or do." I lean over and kiss the top of her head, then walk out with the detectives.

About twenty minutes later, my sister and her cohort are carted off to a Houston jail. I feel nothing but relief. "I'm calling it a day," I tell her. There's enough staff here to make sure everything is okay. I only came in to deal with the break-in.

"Maybe we should talk to Amelia about this."

"Let's save it for another time. Right now, I want to go home and make love to you and forget the past hour."

"Lead the way," she tells me, swatting my ass before we exit my office.

"You're in trouble for that, woman."

Chapter Nine

Tracy

He tosses me onto the bed, and I'm giggling all the way down. He needs this. We need this. He lifts his shirt over his head, dropping it to the floor. I love his body. It's so sexy and full of muscles. "Strip, woman."

I lazily slide my jeans down my legs and then I raise my top over my head, taking my time. I can't see him, but I hear him growl. A laugh escapes me. I finally take it off, and just as I do, he's on top of me, his mouth crashing into mine. Thrusting his hands into my hair, we fall back onto the pillows.

He pulls away from our kiss but grinds his cock onto my pussy. It's then that I notice that while I was teasing him, he had taken off the rest of his clothes. His thickness rubs against my soaked panties.

I want him in me now before I scream. My hips rock up into his, hoping that he'll take me, but instead, he takes his strong hands and runs them down my body. One cups my ass, while the other caresses my entrance. The material that rests between his fingers and my heat adds an extra sense of pleasure. His thumb dips under the fabric and slips into my cunt. I'm gushing with need. Then he presses a pad onto my clit. I'm on the edge.

"I need you now, Derek," I plead. He smiles down at me, then pushes my panties to the side and thrusts into me.

"Is that what you need?" he asks, taking long strokes inside.

"Yes, give it to me, Sheriff."

"Fuck, baby. You're going to make me come quick talking like that," he mutters, grabbing my breasts, then bending down to take one into his mouth.

I wrap my legs around his waist. He picks up his pace, grunting and moaning as the headboard slams against the wall. I love the sounds our heated bodies make as our flesh slaps together. I can feel him tense, then I squeeze.

I want all his cum inside of me. The thought is all the push I need to come hard, pulsating and gripping his cock until he gives it all to me. Every stroke of his thickness sends another shiver of pleasure through me, extending my orgasm.

He rests his head on my chest as we get our breathing under control.

"Can we get married tomorrow?" I ask. I want to be his wife more than I can even explain.

"Wow, baby. You're going to make me fuck you again with words like that," he chuckles.

"Well, in that case, I can't wait to be Mrs. Wright," I tease, but the humor is gone from his eyes and a sensual desire crosses his expression.

"I told you about using words like that." He thrusts his hips forward, and we begin our next session with the constant words of love.

Chapter Ten

Derek

One Month Later...

I walk into the bakery looking for Tracy when I see a young man talking to her, smiling and laughing. I want to break his jaw instantly. I make it to the counter and around it without a word. I pull my wife into my arms and slam my mouth to hers. She hesitates for just a second, then joins wholeheartedly. I pull back a few seconds later because I've proven my point. The young man stares nervously like I'm going to kill him, but I just address my wife, "Baby, you almost ready to go home?"

"Just as soon as I'm done helping this customer, I'll be ready."

"Okay, baby." I grab her ass and stand there while the guy who had been flirting with my wife finishes his choices.

As soon as he walks out of the door, she turns to me, slapping my chest. "What's the matter with you, caveman?"

"What? I saw the way he was looking at you."

"I think you're crazy."

"Well, I don't give two shits. I don't want guys' jaws dropping every time you're around."

"They definitely won't be for long," she says, rubbing her belly. It takes me a moment, but then I get it. I pick her up and spin her around, nearly taking out one of the glass counters.

"Oops. Let's get out of here."

"Okay, I'll be ready in a few. Carly and Carter are cleaning up the back." She doesn't enter the kitchen before knocking. I don't have to know what that's about. She told me about walking in on them kissing passionately. Things may have gotten dirtier if she hadn't walked in. Carly and Carter are newly married as well, so they're fucking whenever and wherever they can. That's what I plan to do to celebrate the fact that I filled Tracy with my baby.

"Thank you, Tracy," Carter says, coming out to lock up. "Hey, Sheriff. How's it going?"

"It's going great. I'm on cloud motherfucking nine right now. You?"

"I will be too when I get my woman home," Carter remarks. He's a doctor who's moving his practice to town to be close to her business. He's a good guy and obsessed with her like I am with Tracy.

"Have a good night," I tell him, walking out of the shop with my wife. We wave them off and head home.

The entire drive home, I'm smiling brightly. By the time we get to the house, my sweet wife is sleeping. I carry my little family inside, then tuck them into bed. This is just as good. I surrender to sleep.

Epilogue

Tracy

"I need you to come right now. I'm having the baby," I cry out over the phone. My belly hasn't stopped cramping for the last few hours, but he's been at work all day.

"I'm on my way, sweetheart. I'll be there in ten minutes. Hang in there for me, please, baby." I hear the nervous panic in his voice as he tries to calm me down. I love him even more for it.

"I will," I grunt out. "Ouch," I say, ending the call as the pain gets to me. I might drive myself to the hospital if he doesn't get here soon. Everything is packed and by the door. I try to sit down, but a painful cramp hits me, forcing me back up on my feet. I walk outside, searching for any kind of air I can get. It's November and the weather is a little chilly, but being in Texas, it's still pretty warm compared to up north. The breeze hits me, and I feel ten times better. I hear the sirens in the background over the sound of my own tears. This sucks terribly.

He was supposed to be off, but one of the guys came down with the flu and he was needed for backup. He's already told me he's hiring three more patrol officers. Crime has gone down since the rash of burglaries ended with the capture of a group of teens. Now, staffing is a matter of getting people to shift out for each other. Right now, there's only five of them and even though our town is small, they are still several petty crimes that they have to take care of every day.

Derek pulls in quickly. I hold on to the railing and go down the few stairs, leaving the bags on the steps because I know that he'll be mad if I try to grab them. "I got you, baby. I got you." He scoops me up into his arms and carries me to the car. Instantly the pain feels like it's gone away, even if I know that it's going to be back in a second. I know I have him by my side now. "Okay, let's get you seated right. I love you, baby. And I can't wait to meet our son."

"Me either."

"Just give me one second while I grab our bags, babe." He grabs them, and we fly out toward the highway and to the hospital. Thank heavens he's got the squad car. We were there in less than ten minutes and they are checking me in within the next five.

Every labored breath is only eased with him holding my hand. His phone goes off and he answers, "Hey, pumpkin. Tracy and I are at the hospital right now." He smiles up at me as he talks to Amelia.

"Yay! We're having our baby now," she cries on the other end. "We will be there as soon as we can. So excited," she squeals. I can hear her from the bed.

A small laugh escapes me as he ends the call. "I guess you know she's coming." I nod because another pain hits me just then. Derrick dashes to my side, holding my hand. "I love you so much, Tracy. You're all I can ever think about."

"I love..." A pain rips through me this time, and it's deeper than the last one.

"I'll get the doctor." A nurse nearly collides with him as he opens the door.

"She's in pain."

"Yes, sir. We know. Her sensors went off at our desk." Derek returns to my side, and the woman sits on the bed between my legs after putting on some gloves. "Mrs. Wright, I need to check you. Just relax as best you can." She lifts the covers and drops them fast. "Oh heavens, it's time for the doctor." She jumps up and calls for the doctor. It's then they prepare for the actual delivery. Derek squeezes my hand and kisses my brow. I look at him and suddenly, I'm a bit ticked off.

Twenty minutes later, I'm giving out the final painful push of my son's broad shoulders.

"You did it," he says as our son cries out in the room.

They lay my little man on my chest. He's not so little. He goes from my chin to my crotch. I can't believe he fit inside me. "He's beautiful," I sob, kissing his head. Derek kisses both of our foreheads, and I can see the tears in his eyes.

"Sorry, I have to get him cleaned up." The nurse takes him from us.

"He's perfect, my lovely wife." He kisses my lips this time. "Thank you for giving me a son."

"I couldn't have done it without you by my side, Derek," I tell him.

"You weren't saying that about five minutes ago." I shrug in embarrassment. I was kind of a total bitch.

"I'm sorry. I shouldn't have been so mean," I apologize.

He brushes my stray hairs away from my face, then runs his fingers down my cheek. "I'm not bothered. Baby, I know that I wouldn't like the person who has my body being ripped in two. I'm sorry that you had to go through so much."

"I love you, Derek," I whisper, looking into his happy face.

"My love for you knows no bounds, Tracy."

Derek

A year later...

"Amelia, are you ready?" I ask my daughter. I know this is hard for her, but there are some things that need to be done. She nods, holding Blake's hand. We go into the coroner's office in Houston to make the ID. A week before her trial, she got enough heroin to send her over. She overdosed, and now it's our job to handle the identification even though they know it's her.

The viewing will only take a moment. Since Amelia has only seen her once, she didn't need to be here, but she wanted to see her—as if to say a final goodbye. We're in and out of the glassed window viewing area.

"Are you okay, pumpkin?" I ask her. She throws herself into my arms, crying softly.

"Yes, I am fine. It's sad that she did this to herself. I know she's partly a victim of circumstance, but she lost out on so much because of it. I feel sorry for her and for you."

"Pumpkin, thank you for being the woman I'd hoped

you'd be. I'm sad for her, but I lost her a very long time ago. I'm sorry that you missed out on having a normal life."

"I had a pretty normal one. You're the one just starting over."

"I'm happy with that though. I got you and Tracy in the process. I call that a win. Now come on. Let's get back home so Tracy isn't too worried."

"You did good. Stalking her worked out well for all of us." We drive back to Palace and try to let the pain stay back in Houston. As soon as I see Tracy, everything is washed away. The pain, sadness, and sacrifice are all worth the love I found in her.

Derek

Twenty-Four Years Later...

"That smells so damn good, baby," I murmur against her ear. "And so do you," he continues, sliding his nose up and down my neck. A moan escapes my lips.

"Dad," Jason, our youngest, complains.

"You don't like me showing your mom the affection she deserves, then leave the room," I tell him with my arms around Tracy's waist.

In comes Frank, our oldest, who has just come back from another tour of duty. "Bro, when are you going to learn that they're never going to stop."

"Tell me about it, but damn, I'm about to eat."

"It's okay. More for me." Tracy hands me a plate. This is my second favorite breakfast. My first has been limited to our bedroom while the kids are home on vacation.

"Hey, I didn't say I wasn't going to eat."

"Then quit bitching," Frank barks out. He opens the fridge and pulls out some juice. My boy has got some issues that I want him to work through. Maybe I can get him to take my place as a local top cop. I've held the sheriff position for over thirty-two years, and eight years in law enforcement before that. I'm past ready to retire. I want more time with Tracy. Our town managed to stay small and primarily fairly safe.

"What's up your ass, Frankenstein?" I look at my son and know exactly what it's about. He's got a crush on a girl. The last I heard, she's on vacation and won't be back before he leaves again.

"Drop it, Jason." Ellen, my second oldest, comes into the kitchen. Krista comes into the kitchen after her. We have four kids, and they are all over eighteen now.

"We have three more weeks of vacation. I want to have a barbecue before you all leave," I tell them. We're in Texas after all; barbecues are a must.

"Then we have about two weeks. I've got to report back. I don't know for how long at the moment, but I'm not going to be back before they go back," Frank adds.

"I say this weekend would be perfect," Ellen remarks, giving her mother a suspicious look. I know that it's better to stay out of it. At twenty-one, I don't want to picture my daughter as anything but the little girl who used to sit on my lap and thought I was the best daddy in the world.

We all finish our breakfast, but all my mind wanders to is my wife's spectacular ass. She's been feeling old lately. I told her we're both getting older, and I'm a fuck ton older than her. Damn, I find her sexy as fuck. I run my tongue over my bottom lip, then bite it. I've been salivating over it since the day we met. I want my hands on her every chance we get. Over the years, it's gotten harder because of the kids and work. But when we do, age has nothing on our fucking. I'm going to need to remind all the fuckers at the barbeque to keep their eyes to themselves. She's mine and always will be. She's aged like a fine wine in an hourglass.

"Mrs. Wright, I'd love to have a word with you—alone," I whisper in her ear. The kids get up and make excuses to leave the house today. In twenty minutes, the dishes are done and all four are out to the movies. Fuck, yeah, I don't wait for her to turn away from the sink. I press my body against hers, rubbing my hard cock on her. I'm sixty, but this woman makes me feel like I'm thirty-six all over again. "I want to fuck you right here, right now," I say, biting on her shoulder. She throws her head back, moaning and grinding her ass on my cock.

"Hey," Frank calls out. Damn it, I hold my body still against Tracy's. "Shit, you couldn't wait until we drove away?"

"What's up? Did you forget something?"

"Yeah, the keys to your truck." He snatches them off the hook and is out the door again.

"Let's go up to our room. Then you can do me in privacy."

"Damn it, a few more weeks and we're going to be all alone. Then I'm going to fuck you on every surface in this damn place," I grumble. I grab her around the waist and then flip her over my shoulder, stalking up the stairs to our bedroom.

"Let's do this, old man." She swats my ass, but I return the favor. And a lot more.

About the Author

Find me on:
Website/Newsletter: www.cmsteele.com
Amazon Author Page: www.amazon.com/C-M-Steele/e/B00MQ9FPZS/
Facebook: www.facebook.com/CMsteele2014
TikTok: www.tiktok.com/@authorcmsteele
Instagram: https://www.instagram.com/c.m._steele/
Twitter: https://twitter.com/Author_CMSteele
Bookbub: https://www.bookbub.com/authors/c-m-steele

Also by C.M. Steele

A Best Friends Duet:

Picture Perfect * Instant Obsession

Best Friends Series:

Always You * His Dirty Secret * Sleep Tight

Bianchi Crime Family:

Married to the Mob * Captured by the Mob * Owned by the Mob

Cavanaugh Security Series:

Protecting Macy * Securing Blake

The Cline Brothers of Colorado:

Whatever it Takes * Taking Whatever He Wants * Finding Paradise

The Conti Crime Family Series:

Alessio * Dario * Enrico * Matteo

Dirty Boss Series:

My Pet * My Cookie * My Flower * My Valentine

(Now on Audio)

The Falling Hard & Fast Series:

Falling for the Boss * Falling for the Enemy * Falling Hard

The Fiore Family:

Christmas with the Beast * Christmas with the Boss * Christmas with the Sheriff

Gimme Series:

Sugar * Luck * Rain * Cream * Heat * Love

Holly Hills Christmas:

Holiday's Cookies * Celeste's Secret * Bethany's Crush

The James Family:

No Choice * No Way Out * No More Waiting

Keepsakes:

Keeping Blossom * Keep in Mind

The Lamian Wars:

Bound * Reveal * Release

All Hallows Eve

The Middleton Hotels:

Built for Me * Built to Last * Built Strong

Built Over Time * Built Overnight

Nothing but Trouble Series:

Taking the Bait * Taking the Mafia Princess

The O'Connell Family:

Claiming Red * Burning for Claire

Claiming Abby * Reminding Red

Obsessed Alpha Series:

Stone * Cole * Graham

Theo * Maddox * Alessandro

Tony * Cormack * Cameron * Jake

Reynolds Ranch Series:

Lara * Tobias

A Rocky Start Series:

Rocky Waters * Her Rock * Rocky Start

A Rough Hands Novella:

My Miracle * Nailing my Wife

Say Something Series:

Say Uncle * Say Please * Say Uncle: Doggy Style

Second Generation:

Say Yes

Sister Switch:

Testing Her Professor * Assisting Her Boss

A Steele Christmas:

Mason's Winter * Perfectly Wrapped * The Company You Keep

A Steele Fairy Tale:

My Gold * My Forever * My Property * My Prince Charming

A Steele Riders Family Novella Series:

Sammie * Roxie * Mike

Steele Riders MC Series:

Boomer * Mick * Jackson * Doc * Beast * Ghost

Wrench * Blade * Boss * Cowboy * Law *Cyber

Southern Hospitality:

Down South * Gone South

Sweet Temptation Bay:

A Taste Of Honey

Sweetheart's Treats:

Sweet Surprise * Doctor's Orders, Sweetheart * Sweet Surrender

Twin Sin:

Stalk Me Please * Sinful Intent

White Wolf Ridge Series:

Turner

Wolfe Creek Series:

Wolfe's Den * Beta: Her Alpha

Raging Kane * Written in History

Standalones:

Buying Love * Conquering Alexandria * Ecstasy Captured

Grant's Deal * In Heat * Intense

Killer Abs * Love Discovered * Loving My Neighbor * Lucky Ride

Mrs. Valentine * My Christmas Gift

Rainy Days * Stormy Nights * Red Hot Nights

Room Service * Scarred * Sharp Curves

So Wrong * Standing There

The Mobster's Virgin * The Wedding Guest * Unexpected

www.ingramcontent.com/pod-product-compliance
Lightning Source LLC
LaVergne TN
LVHW090939080826
845145LV00003B/815

9781954645110